WILLIAM SHAKESPEARE'S

JULIUS CAESAR

CAMPFIRE®

KALYANI NAVYUG MEDIA PVT LTD

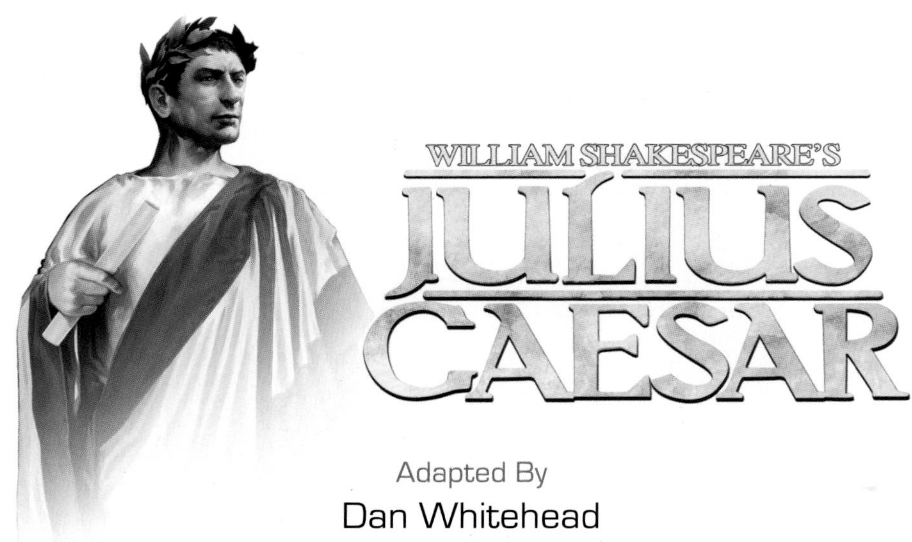

Adapted By

Dan Whitehead

Edits

Parama Majumder, Jason Quinn, Aadithyan Mohan

Line Art

Naresh Kumar

Color

Vijay Sharma & Pradeep Sherawat

Desktop Publishing

Bhavnath Chaudhary

Cover Art

Lalit Kumar Sharma & Pradeep Sherawat

www.campfire.co.in

Mission Statement

To entertain and educate young minds by creating unique illustrated books that recount stories of human values, arouse curiosity in the world around us, and inspire with tales of great deeds of unforgettable people.

Published by Kalyani Navyug Media Pvt Ltd
101 C, Shiv House, Hari Nagar Ashram, New Delhi 110014, India

ISBN: 978-93-80741-80-2

Printed in India

JULIUS CAESAR
CASSIUS
CALPURNIA
BRUTUS
MARK ANTONY
OCTAVIUS

ACT I, SCENE I

Rome, 44 B.C.

For five years a bloody civil war had raged, as 10 the Great fought for control of Rome against his former ally, the legendary general Julius Caesar.

But Pompey's forces were no match for the man whose military cunning expanded Roman rule into Gaul and Britain. After a bitter defeat at the Battle of Pharsalus, Pompey fled to Egypt where he was betrayed and assassinated.

Caesar returned to Rome as its sole, undisputed ruler; and the city celebrated his victory.
But not all Romans were pleased to see him return...

Flavius and Marullus were two Roman tribunes who were responsible for keeping peace in Rome. To defy them was strictly forbidden. They did not welcome Caesar's return at all.
Home, you idle creatures, get you home. Is this a holiday? Speak, what trade art thou?

Why, sir, a carpenter.
Where is thy leather apron and thy rule? What dost thou with thy best apparel on?

You, sir, what trade are you?
A mender of bad soles. I beseech you, sir, be not out with me; yet if you be out, sir, I can mend you.
What meanest thou by that? Mend me, thou saucy fellow!

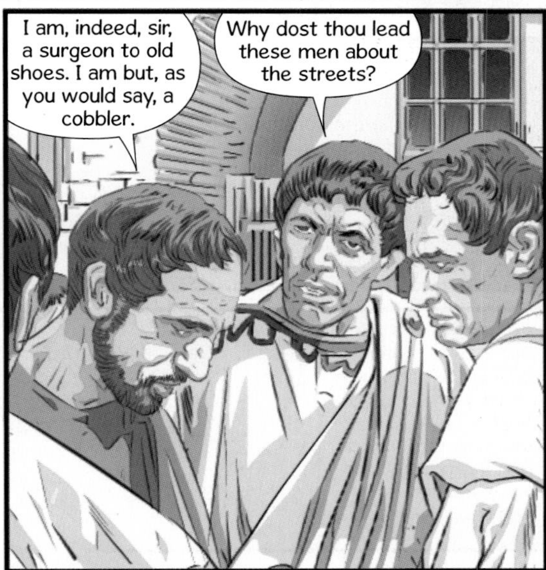
I am, indeed, sir, a surgeon to old shoes. I am but, as you would say, a cobbler.
Why dost thou lead these men about the streets?

Indeed, sir, we make holiday, to see Caesar, and to rejoice in his triumph.

Wherefore rejoice? What conquest brings he home?
You worse than senseless things! O you hard hearts, you cruel men of Rome...
Knew you not Pompey? Do you now strew flowers in his way that comes in triumph over Pompey's blood?
Run to your houses, fall upon your knees, pray to the gods to intermit the plague that needs must light on this ingratitude.
They vanish tongue-tied in their guiltiness. Go you down that way towards the Capitol; this way will I. Disrobe the images, if you do find them deckt with ceremonies.
May we do so, Flavius? You know it is the feast of Lupercal*
It is no matter; let no images be hung with Caesar's trophies. These growing feathers pluckt from Caesar's wing will make him fly an ordinary pitch; who else would soar above the view of men, and keep us all in servile fearfulness.

*An ancient Roman festi
of purification and fertili

ACT I, SCENE II
Citizens lined the streets of Rome to witness Caesar's triumphant procession.
Make way! Make way!

Calpurnia, my wife.
Here, my lord.
Stand you directly in Mark Antony's way, when he doth run his course.
As you wish, my lord.
Caesar's friend and fellow general Mark Antony was to run the race for the feast of Lupercal. Touching people as one ran was said to bring good luck.
Forget not in your speed, Antonius, to touch Calpurnia; for our elders say, the barren, touched in this holy chase, shake off their sterile curse.
I shall remember. When Caesar says 'Do this', it is perform'd.

*March 15 of the Roman calendar.

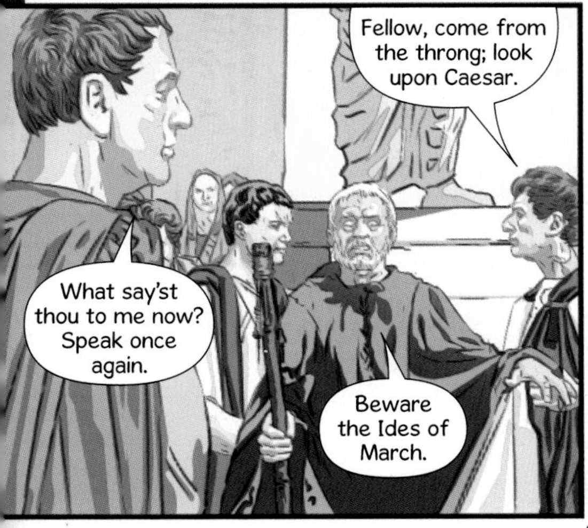

As Caesar's procession moved on, Cassius and Brutus, members of the Roman Senate and two of Caesar's most trusted advisors, stayed behind.
Brutus, will you go see the order of the course?
Not I. I am not gamesome.
Brutus's father had been killed by Pompey, and although he did not always agree with Caesar, he respected and loved him as a friend.
However, he feared that with nobody to oppose him, Caesar might become a tyrant.
I do lack some part of that quick spirit that is in Antony. Let me not hinder your desires; I'll leave you.
Cassius was Brutus's brother-in-law and also a close friend. He had few doubts that Caesar's power would grow out of control, and he already had a plan to prevent that from happening.
But it was not a plan he could carry off alone; so he began recruiting others to his cause...
Brutus, I do observe you now of late. You bear too stubborn and too strange a hand over your friend that loves you.
Let not my good friends construe any further my neglect than that poor Brutus, with himself at war, forgets the shows of love to other men.
Then, Brutus, I have much mistook your passion; by means whereof this breast of mine hath buried thoughts of great value.
Tell me, good Brutus, can you see your face?
No, Cassius, for the eye sees not itself but by reflection from some other thing.
'Tis just; and it is very much lamented, Brutus that you have no such mirrors as will turn your hidden worthiness into your eye, that you migh see your shadow.

Into what dangers would you lead me, Cassius, that you would have me seek into myself for that which is not in me?
Good Brutus, since you know you cannot see yourself so well as by reflection, I, your glass, will modestly discover to yourself that of yourself which you yet know not of.
But before he could continue, the shouts from Caesar's procession interrupted Cassius's speech...
CAESAR! CAESAR! CAESAR!
What means this shouting? I do fear the people choose Caesar for their king...
Ay, do you fear it? Then must I think you would not have it so?
I would not, Cassius; yet I love him well.
What is it that you would impart to me? If it be aught toward the general good, set honor in one eye, and death in the other, and I will look on both indifferently; for let the gods so speed me as I love the name of honor more than I fear death.
Well, honor is the subject of my story. I cannot tell what you and other men think of this life; but for my single self, I had as lief not be as live to be in awe of such a thing as I myself. I was born free as Caesar; so were you: we both have fed as well...

We can both endure the winter's cold as well as he, for once upon a raw and gusty day, the troubled Tiber chafing with her shores, Caesar said to me...
Darest thou, Cassius, now leap in with me into this angry flood, and swim to yonder point?
I plunged in, and bade him follow. So, indeed, he did.
The torrent roar'd; and we did buffet it with lusty sinews. But ere we could arrive the point proposed, Caesar cried...
Help me, Cassius, or I sink!
I, as Aeneas, our great ancestor, did from the flames of Troy upon his shoulder the old Anchises bear, so from the waves of Tiber did I the tired Caesar.
And this man is now become a god; and Cassius must bend his body, if Caesar carelessly but nod on him.
He had a fever when he was in Spain, and, when the fit was on him, I did mark how he did shake. 'Tis true, this god did shake!
Ye gods, it doth amaze me, a man of such a feeble temper should so get the start of the majestic world, and bear the palm alone.

A roar from the crowd distracted the pair...
CAESAR!
I do believe that these applauses are for some new honors that are heapt on Caesar.
He doth bestride the narrow world like a Colossus*; and we petty men walk under his huge legs, and peep about to find ourselves dishonorable graves.
Men at some time are masters of their fates. The fault, dear Brutus, is not in our stars, but in ourselves that we are underlings.
*A giant statue of the Greek sun god, Helios, which once straddled the harbor of Rhodes in Greece.
Brutus, and Caesar! Why should that name be sounded more than yours?
That you do love me, I am nothing jealous; what you would work me to, I have some aim. What you have said I will consider.
Till then, my noble friend, chew upon this – Brutus had rather be a villager than to repute himself a son of Rome under these hard conditions.
I am pleased my simple words have lit a fire in you, dear friend. I am glad that my weak words have struck but thus much show of fire from Brutus.

Hush now. The games are done, and Caesar is returning.
Look you, Cassius, the angry spot doth glow on Caesar's brow, and all the rest look like a chidden train.
Casca will tell us what the matter is.
Antonius, let me have men about me that are fat. Yond Cassius has a lean and hungry look; he thinks too much. Such men are dangerous.
Fear him not, Caesar. He is not dangerous. He is a noble Roman, and well given.
I fear him not. Yet if my name were liable to fear, I do not know the man I should avoid so soon as that spare Cassius.
Seldom he smiles, and smiles in such a sort as if he scorn'd his spirit that could be moved to smile at anything. Such men as he be never at heart's ease whiles they behold a greater than themselves.
You pull'd me by the cloak; would you speak with me?
Ay, Casca. Tell us what hath chanced today that Caesar looks so sad.
I should not then ask Casca what had chanced.
Why, you were with him, were you not?
Why, there was a crown offer'd him, and h put it by with the back of his hand, and then the people fell a-shouting.

They shouted thrice. Was
e crown offer'd him thrice?
Ay, marry, was't! I saw Mark Antony offer him a crown—yet 'twas not a crown neither, 'twas one of these coronets—and as I told you he put it by once, but for all that, to my thinking, he would fain have had it.
Then he offered it to him again, then he put it by again, but, to my thinking, he was very loth to lay his fingers off it.
And then he offered it the third time. He put it the third time by. The rabblement hooted and utter'd such a deal of stinking breath because Caesar refused the crown, that it had almost choked Caesar...
...for he swounded, and fell down at it. And for my own part, I durst not laugh, for fear of opening my lips and receiving the bad air.
What, did Caesar swound?
He fell down in the marketplace, and foam'd at mouth, and was speechless.
'Tis very like. He hath the falling-sickness*.
*Epilepsy
No, Caesar hath it not. But you and I, and honest Casca, we have the falling-sickness.

I know not what you mean by that; but, I am sure, Caesar fell down. If the tag-rag people did not clap him and hiss him, as they use to do the players in the theater, I am no true man.

Marry, before he fell down, when he perceived the common herd was glad he refused the crown, he offer'd them his throat to cut. An I had been a man of any occupation, if I would not have taken him at a word, I would I might go to hell among the rogues.

When he came to himself again, he said, if he had done or said anything amiss, he desired their worships to think it was his infirmity. Three or four wenches, where I stood, cried, 'Alas, good soul!' and forgave him with all their hearts.

But there's no need to be taken of them; if Caesar had stabb'd their mothers, they would have done no less.

And after that, he came, thus sad, away?

Ay.

What of Cicero? Did he say anything? Did Cicero say anything?

Ay, he spoke Greek. I could tell you more news too. Marullus and Flavius, for pulling scarfs off Caesar's images, are put to silence. There was more foolery yet, if I could remember it.

Will you dine with me tomorrow, Casca?

Ay, if I be alive, and your mind hold, and your dinner worth the eating. Farewell.

What a blunt fellow is this grown to be! He was quick mettle when he went to school.
So is he now, in execution of any bold or noble enterprise. This rudeness is a source to his good wit, which gives men stomach to digest his words with better appetite.
For this time I will leave you: Tomorrow, if you please to speak with me, I will come home to you; or, if you will, come home to me, and I will wait for you.
I will do so. Till then, think of the world.
Well, Brutus, thou art noble; yet, see, thy honorable mettle may be wrought from that it is disposed.
I will this night, in several hands, in at his windows throw, as if they came from several citizens, writings, all tending to the great opinion that Rome holds of his name; wherein obscurely Caesar's ambition shall be glanced at.
And, after this, let Caesar seat him sure, for we will shake him, or worse days endure.

ACT I, SCENE III
That evening, a terrible storm raged over Rome...
Good even, Casca. Brought you Caesar home? Why are you so breathless? And why stare you so?
Are not you moved, when all the sway of earth shakes like a thing unfirm?
O Cicero, either there is a civil strife in heaven, or else the world, too saucy with the gods, incenses them to send destruction.
Why, saw you anything more wonderful?
A common slave held up his left hand, which did flame and burn like twenty torches joined, and yet his hand, remained unscorched!
Besides, against the Capitol I met a lion who glared upon me and went surly by without annoying me!
And there were a hundred ghastly women, transformed with fear, who swore they saw men, all in fire, walk up and down the streets.
And yesterday the bird of night did sit at noonday upon the marketplace, shrieking!
Indeed, it is a strange time. But men may construe things after their fashion, clean from the purpose of the things themselves.
Comes Caesar to the Capitol tomorrow?
He doth, for he did bid Antonius send word to you he would be there tomorrow.
Good night then, Casca. This disturbed sky is not to walk in.

Casca and Cicero were not the only souls to brave the rain that night. Cassius also walked the streets, unbowed by the storm.
Who's there?
Cassius! What night is this!
Casca, by your voice.
A very pleasing night to honest men.
Who ever knew the heavens menace so?
Those that have known the earth so full of faults. I have bared my bosom to the thunder-stone, and when the cross blue lightning seem'd to open the breast of heaven, I did present myself even in the aim and very flash of it.
But wherefore did you so much tempt the heavens?
You are dull, Casca; and those sparks of life that should be in a Roman you do want, or else you use not. You look pale, and put on fear, and cast yourself in wonder to see the strange impertinence of the heavens.
But if you would consider the true cause why all these things change their natures, you shall find that heaven hath infused them with these spirits to make them instruments of fear and warning unto some monstrous state.
Now could I, Casca, name to thee a man most like this dreadful night, a man no mightier than thyself or me, yet prodigious grown, and fearful as these strange eruptions are.
'Tis Caesar that you mean. Is it not, Cassius?
Let it be who it is, for Romans now have thews and limbs like to their ancestors, but our fathers' minds are dead. Our yoke and sufferance show us womanish.
Indeed! They say the senators tomorrow mean to establish Caesar as a king!

I know where I will wear this dagger then. Cassius from bondage will deliver Cassius.
Therein, ye gods, you make the weak most strong; therein, ye gods, you tyrants do defeat.
Nor stony tower, nor walls of beaten brass, nor airless dungeon, nor strong links of iron, can be retentive to the strength of spirit...
But life, being weary of these worldly bars, never lacks power to dismiss itself. That part of tyranny that I do bear, I can shake off at pleasure.
So can I. So every bondman in his own hand bears the power to cancel his captivity.
And why should Caesar be a tyrant, then? Poor man! I know he would not be a wolf, but that he sees the Romans are but sheep.
O grief, where hast thou led me? I perhaps speak this before a willing bondman.
You speak to Casca, and to such a man that is no tell-tale. Hold, my hand, and I will set this foot of mine as far as who goes farthest.
There's a bargain made. Now know you, Casca, I have moved already some of the noblest-minded Romans to underg with me an enterprise of honorabl dangerous consequence, and the stay for me in Pompey's porch.

Stand close
while, for here
comes one in
haste.
'Tis Cinna. He
is a friend.
Cinna, where
haste you so?
To find out
you. Who's
that?
It is
Casca.
Am I not
stay'd for?
Yes, you are.
O Cassius, if you
could but win the
noble Brutus to
our party...
Be you content. Good
Cinna, take this paper, and
look you lay it in the praetor's
chair; where Brutus may but
find it. And throw this in at his
window. All this done, repair
to Pompey's porch, where
you shall find us.
Come, Casca, you
and I will yet, ere day,
see Brutus at his house.
Three parts of him is
ours already.
O, he sits high in
all the people's hearts, and
that which would appear
offense in us, his countenance,
like richest alchemy, will
change to virtue.
Him and his worth, you
have right well conceited. Let
us go, for it is after midnight,
and, ere day, we will awake
him, and be sure of him.

The storm passed, but the night still hung gray and weary over the home of Brutus...
What, Lucius, ho!
When, Lucius, when? Awake, I say!
Call'd you, my lord?
Get me a taper in my study, Lucius. When it is lighted, come and call me here.
Caesar would be crown'd—how that might change his nature, there's the question. Crown him? And then, I grant, we put a sting in him that he may do danger with.
The abuse of greatness is when it disjoins remorse from power, and to speak truth of Caesar, I have not known when his affections sway'd more than his reason.
But 'tis a common proof that lowliness is young ambition's ladder, when he once attains the upmost round, he then unto the ladder turns his back.
Therefore think him as a serpent's egg and kill him in the shell.

The taper burneth in your closet, sir. I found this paper, thus seal'd up. I am sure it did not lie there when I went to bed.
Is not tomorrow, boy, the Ides of March?
I know not, sir.
Look in the calendar, and bring me word.
'Brutus, thou sleep'st. Awake and see thyself! Speak, strike, redress! Shall Rome stand under one man's awe?'
Am I entreated to speak and strike? Oh Rome, I make thee promise if the redress will follow, thou receivest thy full petition at the hand of Brutus!
Sir, March is wasted in fourteen days.
'Tis good.
KNOCK! KNOCK!
Go to the gate, somebody knocks.

Since Cassius first did whet me against Caesar, I have not slept. Between the acting of a dreadful thing and the first motion, all the interim is like a phantasma or a hideous dream.
Sir, 'tis Cassius at the door, who doth desire to see you.
Is he alone?
No, sir, there are more with him, half their faces buried in their cloaks.
Let 'em enter.
They are the faction. O Conspiracy, shamest thou to show thy dangerous brow by night, when evils are most free? O, then, by day where wilt thou find a cavern dark enough to mask thy monstrous visage?
For if thou put thy native semblance on not Erebus* itself were dim enough to hide thee from prevention.
*A place of darkness in the underworld through which the dead must pass before they reach Hades.
Good morrow, Brutus! Do we trouble you?
I have been awake all night. Know I these men that come along with you?
Yes, every man of them; no man here but honors you and doth wish you had but that opinion of yourself which every noble Roman bears of you. This is...
Trebonius.
Decius Brutus.
Metellus Cimber.
Cinna.
Casca.
They are all welcome.

Give me your hands all over, one by one.

And let us swear our resolution.

No! Not an oath!

If not the face of men, the sufferance of our souls, the time's abuse—if these be motives weak, break off betimes, and every man hence to his idle bed.

But if these, as I am sure they do, bear fire enough to kindle cowards and to steel with valor the melting spirits of women, then, countrymen, what need we any spur, but our own cause to prick us to redress?

What other oath than honesty to honesty engaged that this shall be, or we will fall for it? Do not stain the even virtue of our enterprise to think that our cause or our performance did need an oath.

But what of Cicero? Shall we sound him?
Let us not leave him out.
O, let us have him, for his silver hairs will purchase us a good opinion, and buy men's voices to commend our deeds.
O, name him not. Let us not break with him, for he will never follow any thing that other men begin.

Shall no man else be toucht but only Caesar?

Decius, well urged. I think it is not meet, Mark Antony, so well beloved of Caesar should outlive Caesar. We shall find of him a shrewd contriver so far as to annoy us all.
Our course will seem too bloody, Caius Cassius, to cut the head off, and then hack the limbs. For Antony is but a limb of Caesar. Let's be sacrificers, but not butchers, Caius.
We all stand up against the spirit of Caesar; and in the spirit of men there is no blood. O that we, then, could come by Caesar's spirit, and not dismember Caesar! But, alas, Caesar must bleed for it! Gentle friends, let's kill him boldly, but not wrathfully.
Yet I fear Mark Antony. For in the ingrafted love he bears to Caesar--
If he loves Caesar, all that he can do is to himself – take thought, and die for Caesar.
DONG! DONG! DONG!
Peace! Count the clock.
The clock hath stricken three.
'Tis time to part.
But it is doubtful yet, whether Caesar will come forth today or no, for he is superstitious grown of late. It may be these apparent prodigies, the unaccustomed terror of this night may hold him from the Capitol today.

Never fear that. If he be so resolved, I can o'ersway him, and bring him to the Capitol.

Nay, we will all of us be there to fetch him.
By the eighth hour. Is that the uttermost?
Be that the uttermost, and fail not then.

Caius Ligarius doth bear Caesar hard who rated him for speaking well of Pompey.
Now, good Metellus, go along by him. He loves me well. Send him but hither, and I'll fashion him.

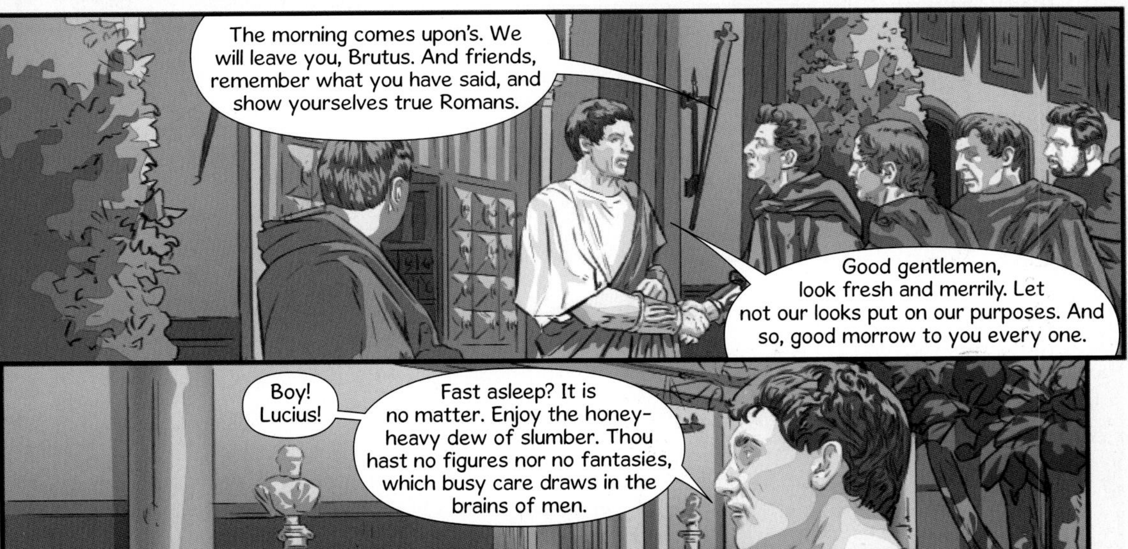

The morning comes upon's. We will leave you, Brutus. And friends, remember what you have said, and show yourselves true Romans.
Good gentlemen, look fresh and merrily. Let not our looks put on our purposes. And so, good morrow to you every one.

Boy! Lucius!

Fast asleep? It is no matter. Enjoy the honey-heavy dew of slumber. Thou hast no figures nor no fantasies, which busy care draws in the brains of men.

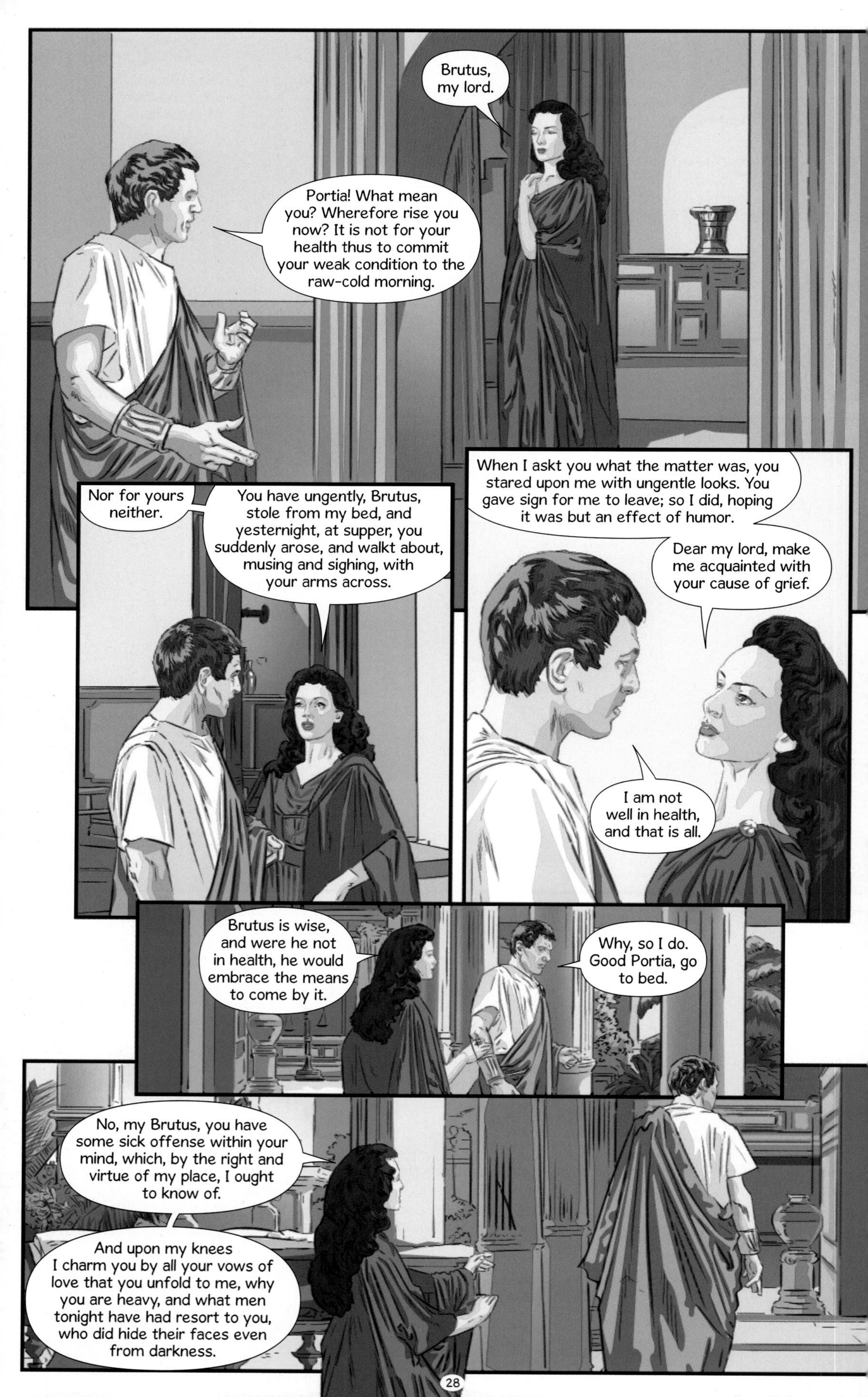
Brutus, my lord.
Portia! What mean you? Wherefore rise you now? It is not for your health thus to commit your weak condition to the raw-cold morning.
Nor for yours neither.
You have ungently, Brutus, stole from my bed, and yesternight, at supper, you suddenly arose, and walkt about, musing and sighing, with your arms across.
When I askt you what the matter was, you stared upon me with ungentle looks. You gave sign for me to leave; so I did, hoping it was but an effect of humor.
Dear my lord, make me acquainted with your cause of grief.
I am not well in health, and that is all.
Brutus is wise, and were he not in health, he would embrace the means to come by it.
Why, so I do. Good Portia, go to bed.
No, my Brutus, you have some sick offense within your mind, which, by the right and virtue of my place, I ought to know of.
And upon my knees I charm you by all your vows of love that you unfold to me, why you are heavy, and what men tonight have had resort to you, who did hide their faces even from darkness.

Kneel not, gentle Portia.
I should not need, if you were gentle Brutus.
You are my true and honorable wife, as dear to me as are the ruddy drops that visit my sad heart.
If this were true, then should I know this secret. Tell me your counsels; I will not disclose 'em.
O ye gods, render me worthy of this noble wife!
One knocks. Portia, go in awhile. And by and by thy bosom shall partake the secrets of my heart.
KNOCK KNOCK
All my engagements I will construe to thee, all the charactery of my sad brows.

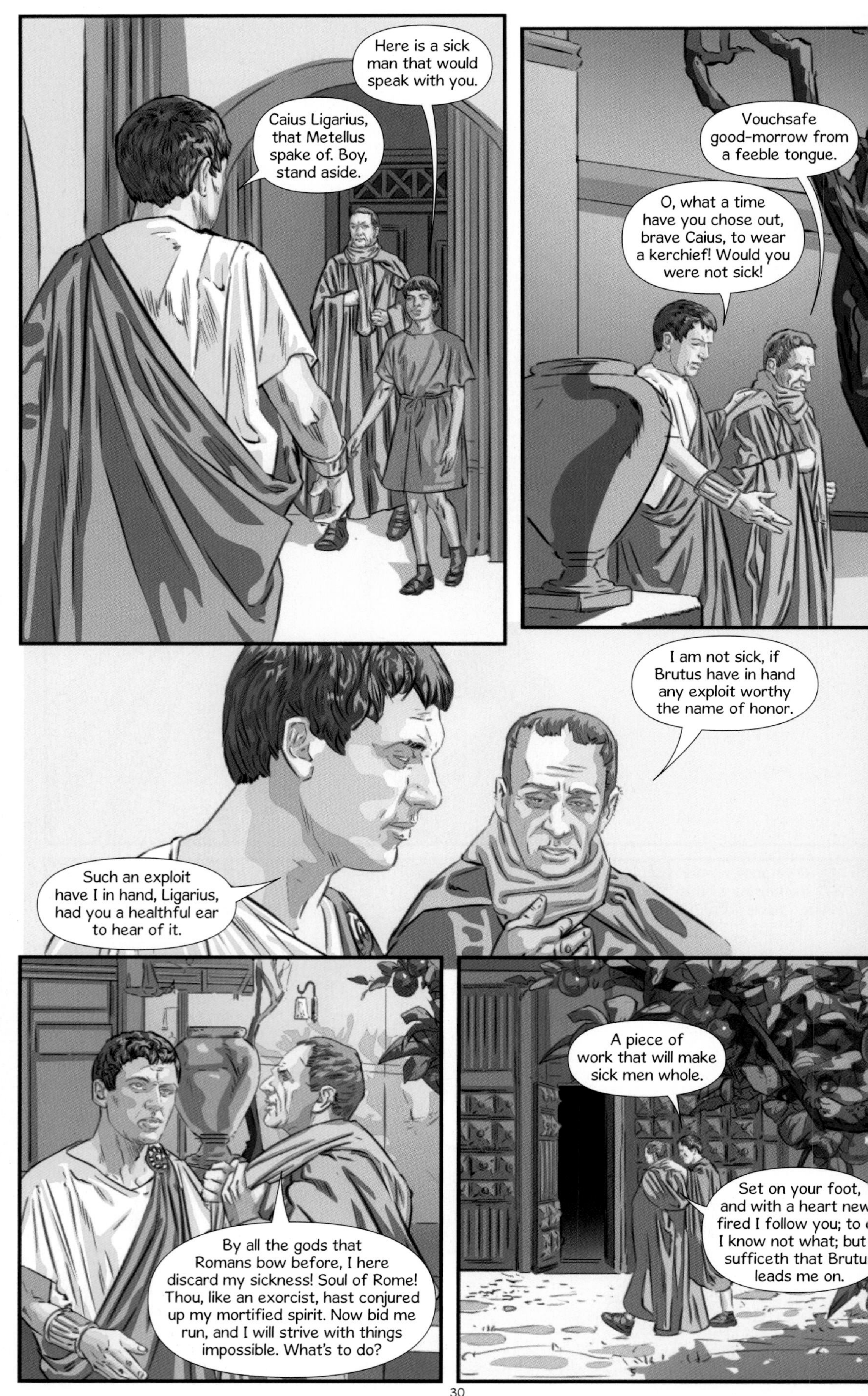

Here is a sick man that would speak with you.
Caius Ligarius, that Metellus spake of. Boy, stand aside.
Vouchsafe good-morrow from a feeble tongue.
O, what a time have you chose out, brave Caius, to wear a kerchief! Would you were not sick!
I am not sick, if Brutus have in hand any exploit worthy the name of honor.
Such an exploit have I in hand, Ligarius, had you a healthful ear to hear of it.
By all the gods that Romans bow before, I here discard my sickness! Soul of Rome! Thou, like an exorcist, hast conjured up my mortified spirit. Now bid me run, and I will strive with things impossible. What's to do?
A piece of work that will make sick men whole.
Set on your foot, and with a heart new fired I follow you; to I know not what; but sufficeth that Brutu leads me on.

ACT II, SCENE II
leanwhile, Caesar restlessly
ced his home, though it was not
storm that kept him awake...
Nor heaven nor earth have been at peace tonight!
Thrice hath Calpurnia in her sleep cried out, 'Help, ho! They murder Caesar!'
Who's within?
My lord?
Go bid the priests do present sacrifice, and bring me their opinions of success.
What mean you, Caesar? Think you to walk forth? You shall not stir out of your house today.
Caesar shall forth! The things that threaten'd me ne'er lookt but on my back; when they shall see the face of Caesar, they are vanished.
Caesar, I never
ood on ceremonies, yet
v they fright me. There
one within who recounts
nost horrid sights seen
by the watch.
A lioness hath whelped in
ne streets; and graves have
awn'd, and yielded up their
ad; fierce fiery warriors fight
on the clouds, which drizzled
blood upon the Capitol.
What can be avoided whose end is purposed by the mighty gods? Yet Caesar shall go forth, for these predictions are to the world in general as to Caesar.
When beggars die,
ere are no comets seen; the
vens themselves blaze forth
the death of princes.
Cowards die many times before their deaths; the valiant never taste of death but once.
Of all the wonders that I yet have heard, it seems to me most strange that men should fear; seeing that death, a necessary end, will come when it will come.

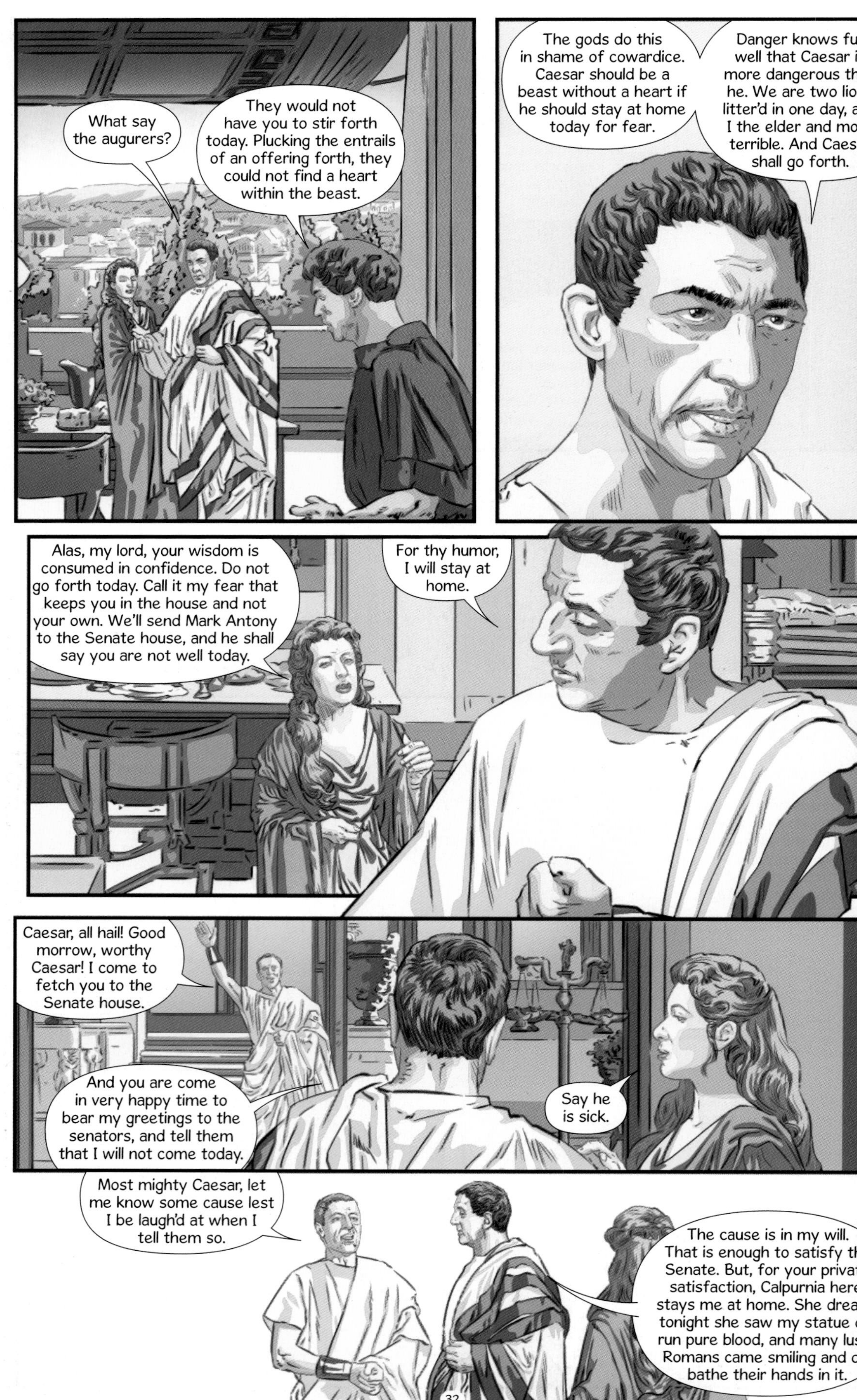
What say the augurers?
They would not have you to stir forth today. Plucking the entrails of an offering forth, they could not find a heart within the beast.
The gods do this in shame of cowardice. Caesar should be a beast without a heart if he should stay at home today for fear.
Danger knows fu well that Caesar i more dangerous th he. We are two lio litter'd in one day, a I the elder and mo terrible. And Caes shall go forth.
Alas, my lord, your wisdom is consumed in confidence. Do not go forth today. Call it my fear that keeps you in the house and not your own. We'll send Mark Antony to the Senate house, and he shall say you are not well today.
For thy humor, I will stay at home.
Caesar, all hail! Good morrow, worthy Caesar! I come to fetch you to the Senate house.
And you are come in very happy time to bear my greetings to the senators, and tell them that I will not come today.
Say he is sick.
Most mighty Caesar, let me know some cause lest I be laugh'd at when I tell them so.
The cause is in my will. That is enough to satisfy th Senate. But, for your priva satisfaction, Calpurnia here stays me at home. She drea tonight she saw my statue run pure blood, and many lus Romans came smiling and d bathe their hands in it.

This dream is all amiss interpreted; it was a vision fair and fortunate. This signifies that from you great Rome shall suck reviving blood, and that great men shall press for tinctures, stains, relics, and recognizance.
And this way have you well expounded it.
The Senate have concluded to give this day a crown to mighty Caesar. If you shall send them word you will not come, their minds may change.
Besides, it were a mock apt to be render'd, for someone to say 'Break up the Senate till another time, when Caesar's wife shall meet with better dreams.'
How foolish do your fears seem now, Calpurnia! I am ashamed I did yield to them. Give me my robe, for I will go.
And look where Publius is come to fetch me.
What, Brutus, are you stirr'd so early too? Good morrow, Casca. Good morrow Caius Ligarius. What is't o'clock?
Caesar, 'tis strucken eight.

See! Antony, that revels long o'nights, is notwithstanding up. Good morrow, Antony.
So to most noble Caesar.
Calpurnia, bid them prepare within.
I have an hour's talk in store for you; be near me, that I may remember you.
Good friends, go in and taste some wine with me, and we like friends will straightway go together.
That every like is not the same, O Caesar, the heart of Brutus yearns to think upon!

CT II, SCENE III

Artemidorus, a humble teacher, had learned of the conspiracy against Caesar and planned to warn him by giving him a letter naming Brutus and Cassius as traitors...
Here will I stand till Caesar pass along, and as a suitor will I give him this.

CT II, SCENE IV

Meanwhile, at the house of Brutus, Portia was worried about her husband...

I prithee, boy, run to the Senate-house; bring me word, boy, if thy lord look well, for he went sickly forth.

And take good note what Caesar doth, what suitors press to him.

Come hither, fellow. Which way hast thou been? Is Caesar yet gone to the Capitol?

Madam, not yet. I go to take my stand, to see him pass on to the Capitol. I have a suit, lady.

If it will please Caesar to be so good as to hear me, I shall beseech him to befriend himself.

Why, know'st thou any harm's intended towards him?

None that I know will be, much that I fear may chance.

O Brutus, the heavens speed thee in thine enterprise!

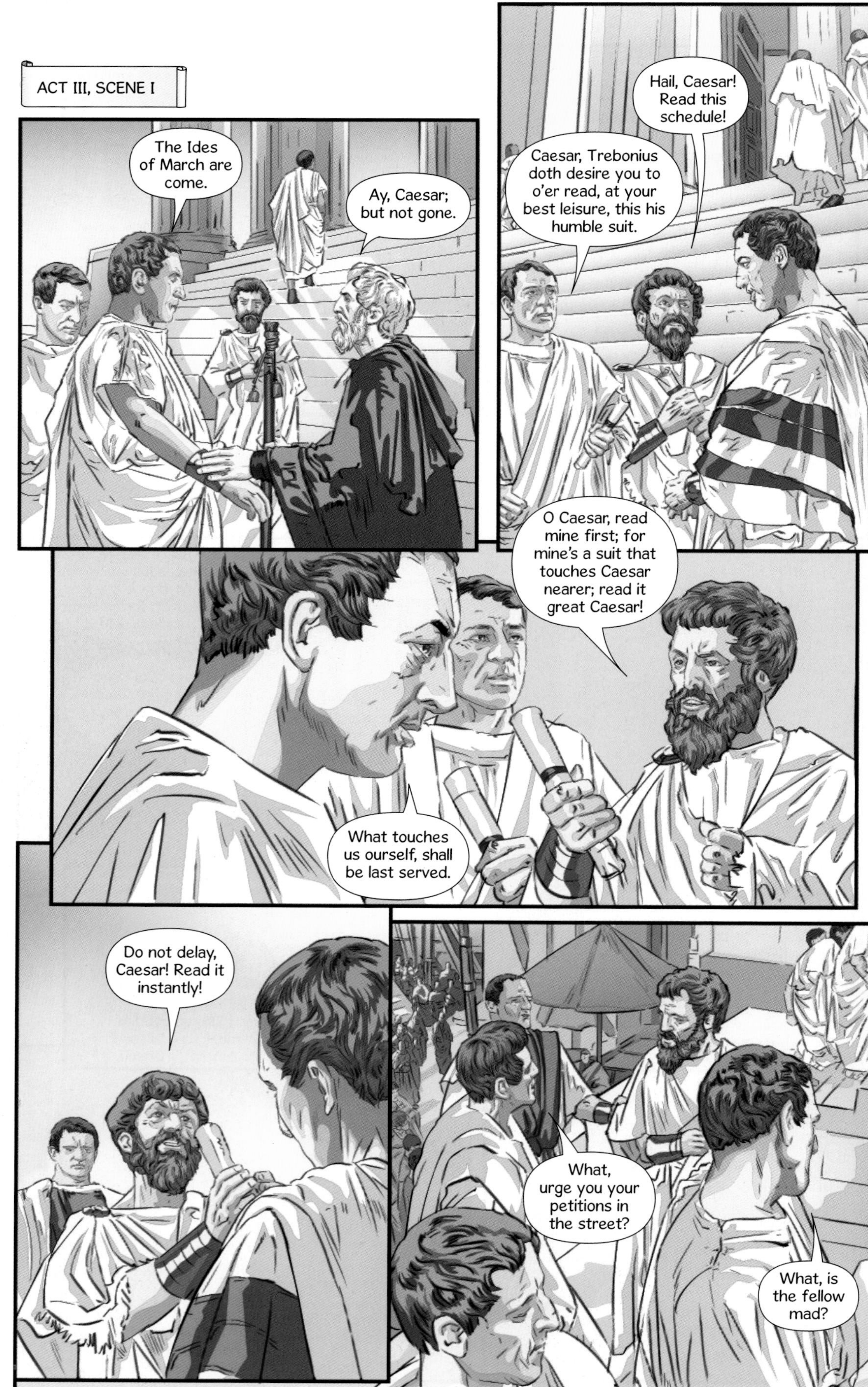
ACT III, SCENE I
The Ides of March are come.
Ay, Caesar; but not gone.
Hail, Caesar! Read this schedule!
Caesar, Trebonius doth desire you to o'er read, at your best leisure, this his humble suit.
O Caesar, read mine first; for mine's a suit that touches Caesar nearer; read it great Caesar!
What touches us ourself, shall be last served.
Do not delay, Caesar! Read it instantly!
What, urge you your petitions in the street?
What, is the fellow mad?

Finally, Caesar reached the Senate, the
eating heart of the Roman Republic, where
itizens could bring their proposals and
etitions to the attention of the ruling class.
I wish your enterprise today may thrive.
What... what enterprise, Popilius?
What said Popilius Lena?
He wisht today our enterprise might thrive.
Look, how he makes to Caesar. Mark him.
Brutus, what shall be done? If this be known, Cassius or Caesar never shall turn back, for I will slay myself.
Cassius, be constant. Popilius Lena speaks not of our purpose, for, look, he smiles, and Caesar doth not change.
Trebonius knows his time; for, look you, Brutus, he draws Mark Antony out of the way.

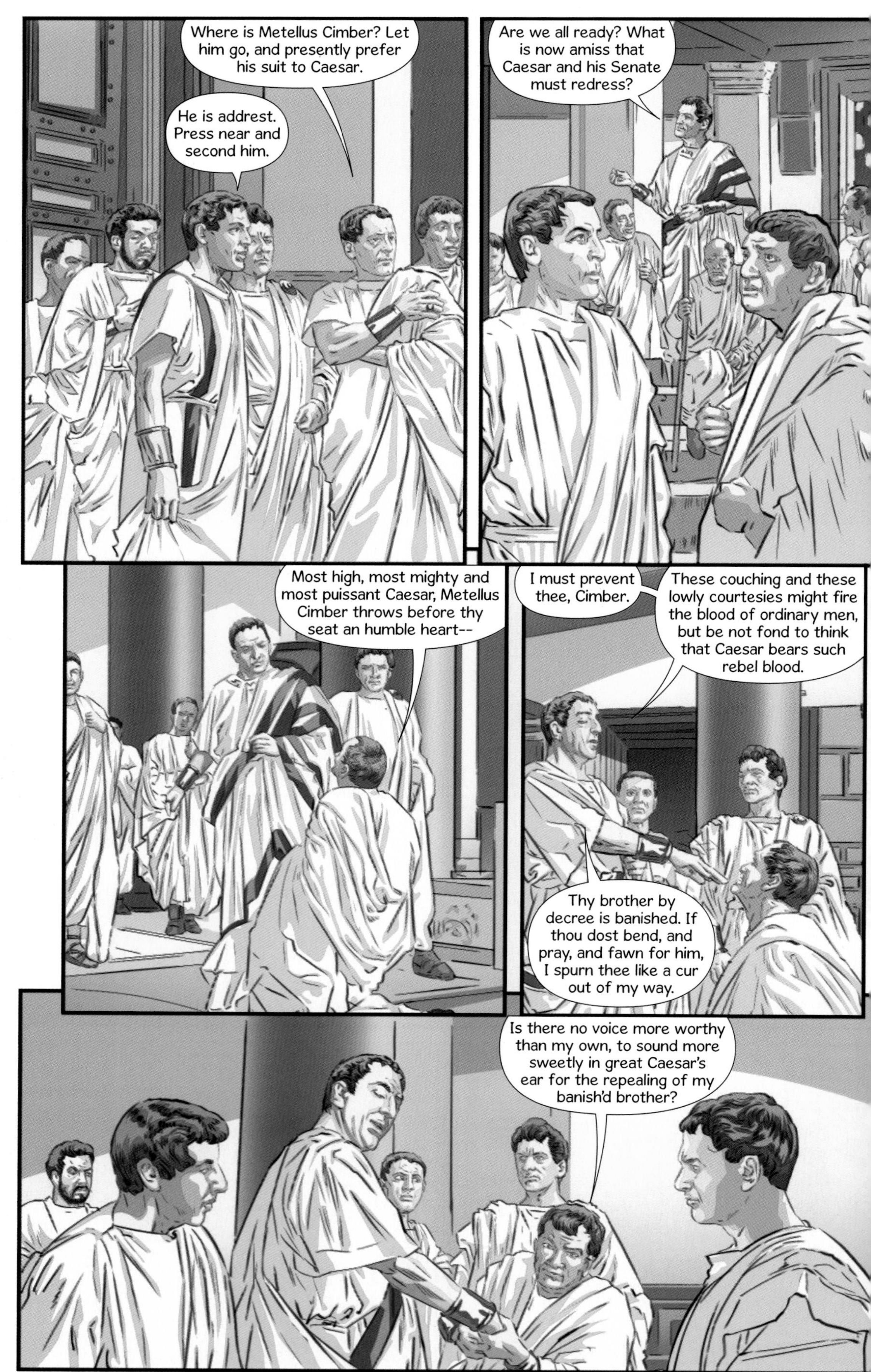
Where is Metellus Cimber? Let him go, and presently prefer his suit to Caesar.
He is addrest. Press near and second him.
Are we all ready? What is now amiss that Caesar and his Senate must redress?
Most high, most mighty and most puissant Caesar, Metellus Cimber throws before thy seat an humble heart--
I must prevent thee, Cimber.
These couching and these lowly courtesies might fire the blood of ordinary men, but be not fond to think that Caesar bears such rebel blood.
Thy brother by decree is banished. If thou dost bend, and pray, and fawn for him, I spurn thee like a cur out of my way.
Is there no voice more worthy than my own, to sound more sweetly in great Caesar's ear for the repealing of my banish'd brother?

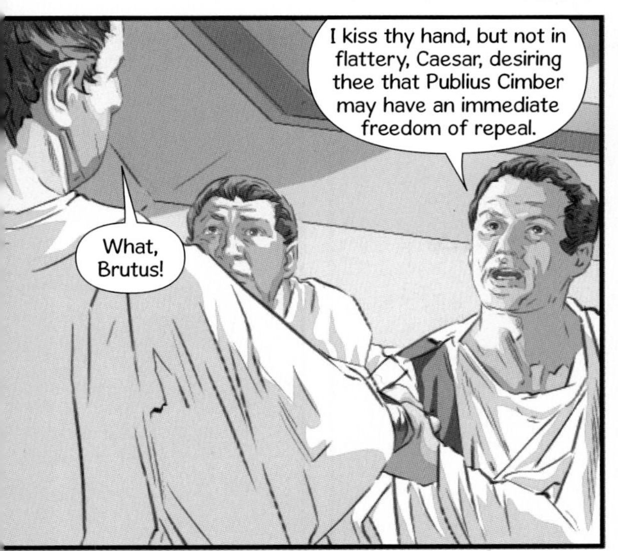

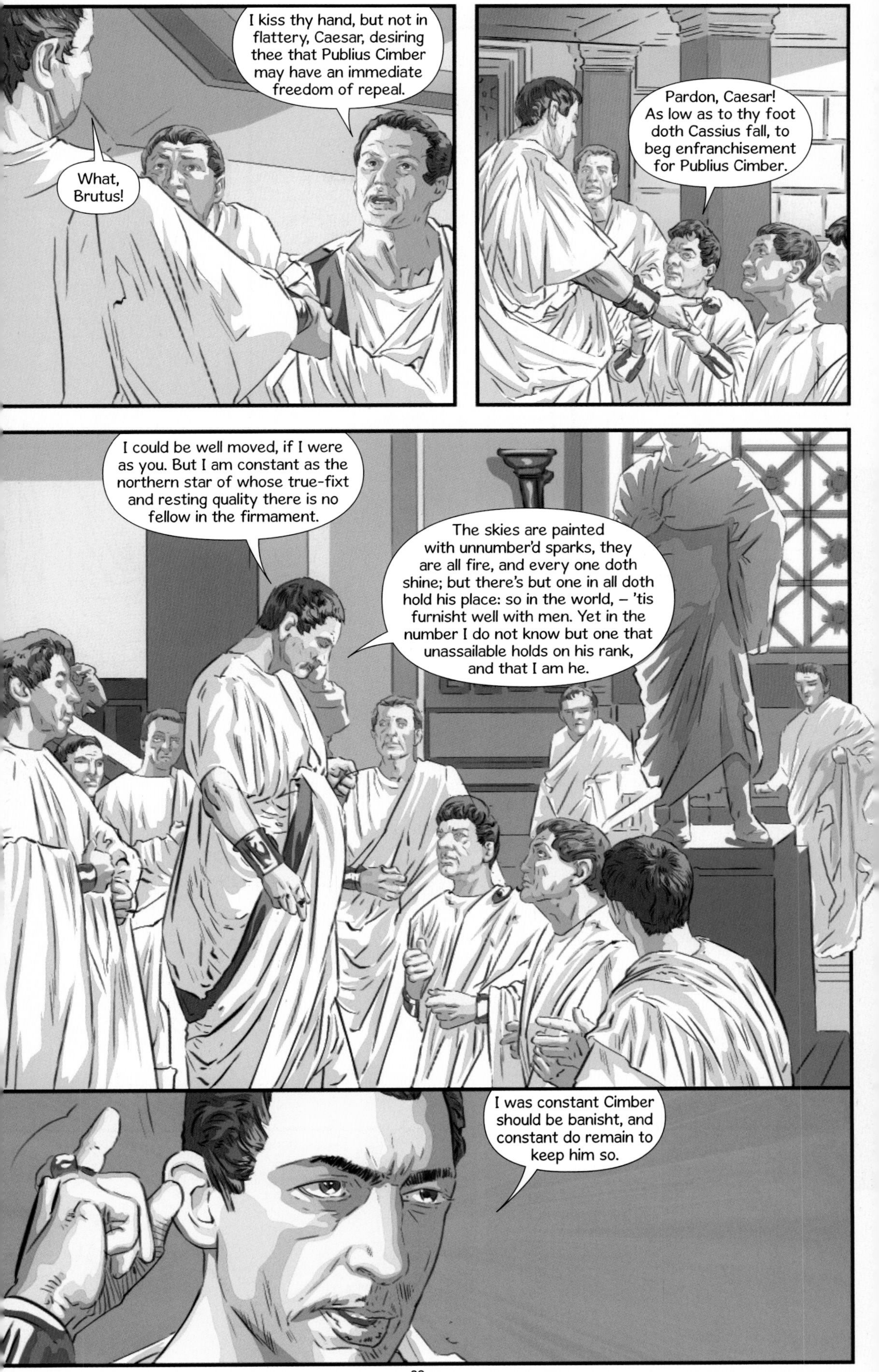

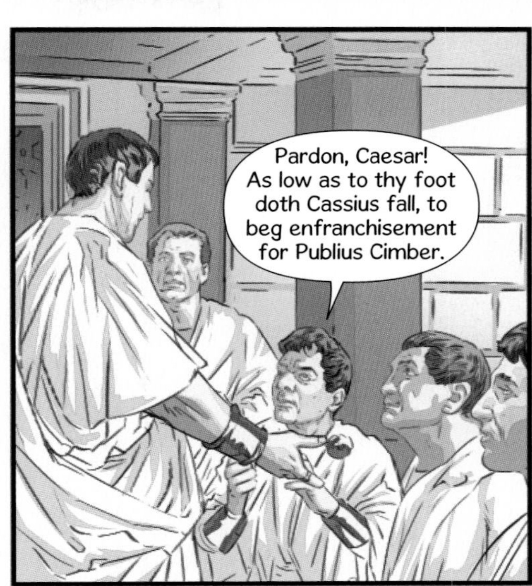

I could be well moved, if I were as you. But I am constant as the northern star of whose true-fixt and resting quality there is no fellow in the firmament.

The skies are painted with unnumber'd sparks, they are all fire, and every one doth shine; but there's but one in all doth hold his place: so in the world, – 'tis furnisht well with men. Yet in the number I do not know but one that unassailable holds on his rank, and that I am he.

I was constant Cimber should be banisht, and constant do remain to keep him so.

Oh Caesar...
Hence! Wilt thou lift up Olympus?
Great Caesar...
Doth not Brutus bootless kneel?
Speak, hands, for me!

s one, the conspirators struck!
Et tu Brute?
Then fall Caesar!
POMPEVS

CLANG!

Liberty! Freedom! Tyranny is dead! Run hence, proclaim, cry it about the streets!
Some to the common pulpits, and cry out, 'Liberty, freedom, and enfranchisement!'
People, and senators, be not affrighted! Fly not, stand still; ambition's debt is paid.
Where is Publius?
Here, quite confounded with this mutiny.
Stand fast together, lest some friend of Caesar's should chance--
Talk not of standing.
Publius, good cheer. There is no harm intended to your person, nor to no Roman else. So tell them, Publius.
And leave us, Publius, lest that the people rushing on us should do your age some mischief.
Do so, and let no man abide this deed, but we the doers.

Trebonius, where is Antony?

Fled to his house amazed. Men, wives, and children stare, cry out, and run as it were doomsday.

Fates, we will know your pleasures. That we shall die, we know; 'tis but the time and drawing days out, that men stand upon.

Why, he that cuts off twenty years of life cuts off so many years of fearing death.

Grant that, and then is death a benefit; so are we Caesar's friends that have abridged his time of fearing death.

Stoop, Romans, stoop, and let us bathe our hands i
Caesar's blood and besmear o
swords; then walk we forth
even to the market-place, an
waving our red weapons o'e
our heads, let's all cry, 'Peace
freedom, and liberty!'

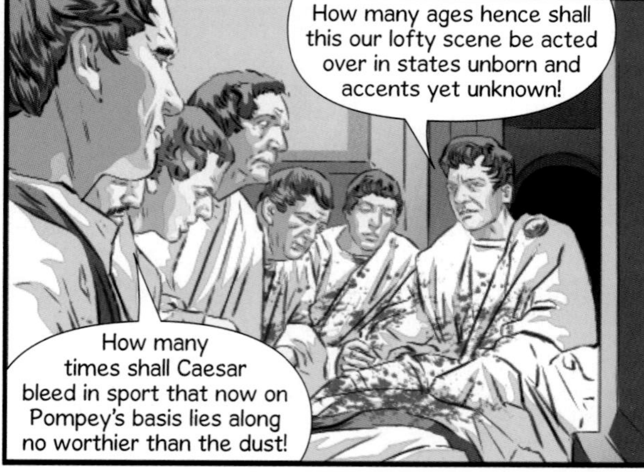

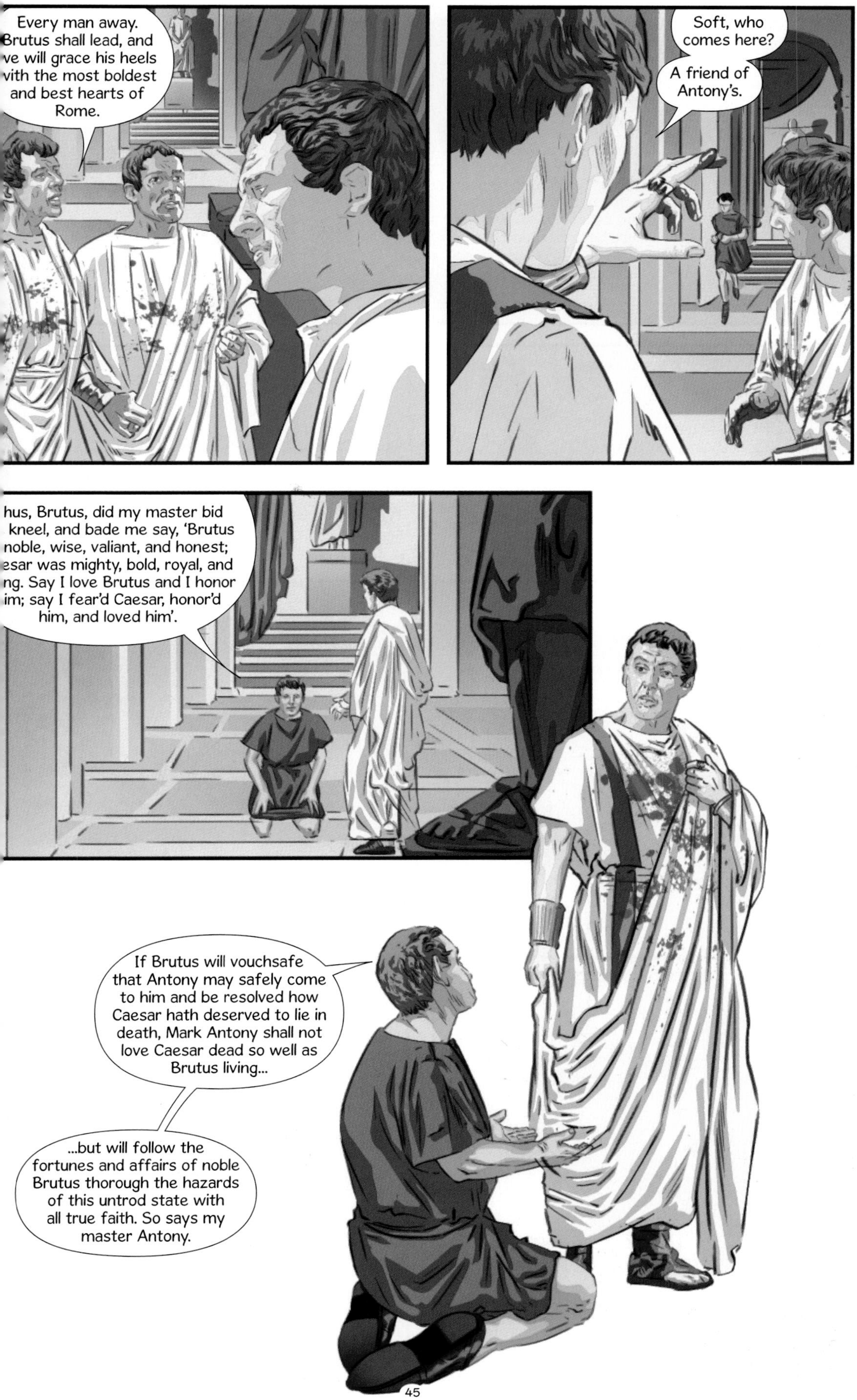

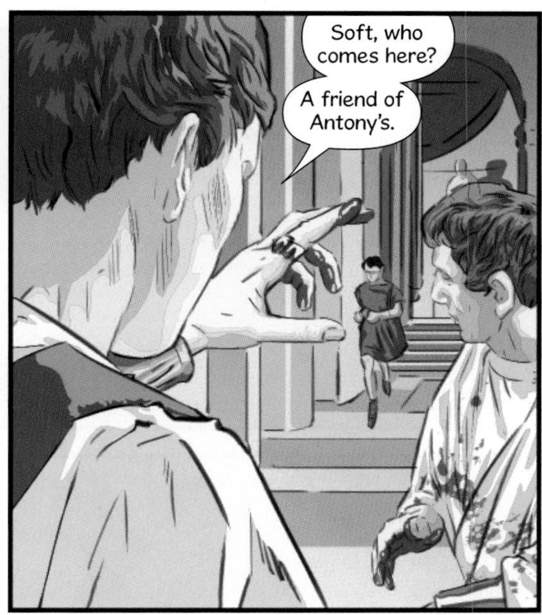

hus, Brutus, did my master bid kneel, and bade me say, 'Brutus noble, wise, valiant, and honest; esar was mighty, bold, royal, and ng. Say I love Brutus and I honor im; say I fear'd Caesar, honor'd him, and loved him'.

If Brutus will vouchsafe that Antony may safely come to him and be resolved how Caesar hath deserved to lie in death, Mark Antony shall not love Caesar dead so well as Brutus living...

...but will follow the fortunes and affairs of noble Brutus thorough the hazards of this untrod state with all true faith. So says my master Antony.

Thy master is a wise and valiant Roman; I never thought him worse. Tell him, so please him come unto this place, he shall be satisfied and, by my honor, depart untouch'd.
I'll fetch him presently.

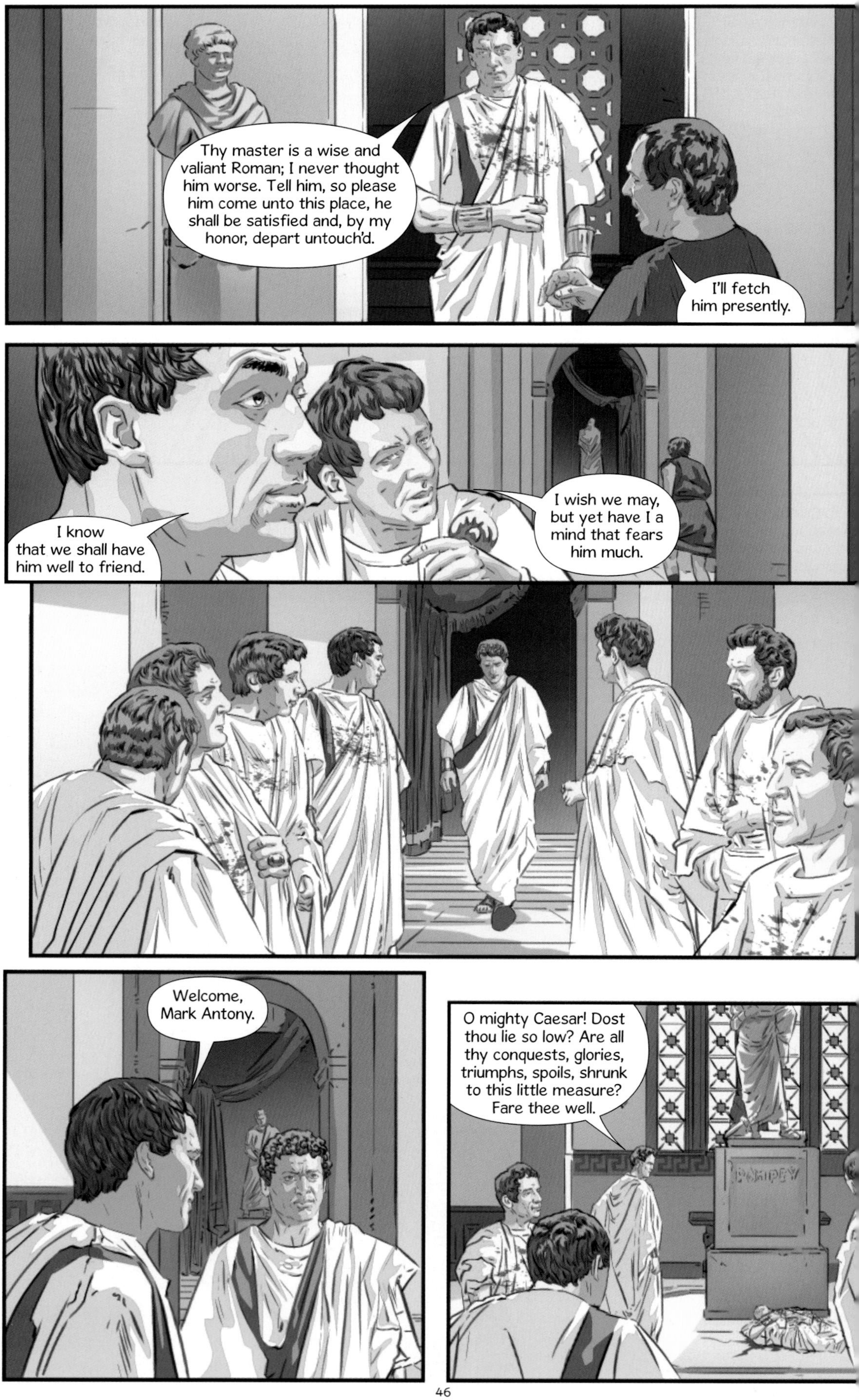

I know that we shall have him well to friend.

I wish we may, but yet have I a mind that fears him much.

Welcome, Mark Antony.

O mighty Caesar! Dost thou lie so low? Are all thy conquests, glories, triumphs, spoils, shrunk to this little measure? Fare thee well.

I know not, gentlemen, what you intend, who else must be let blood, who else is rank.
If I myself, there is no hour so fit as Caesar's death's hour, nor no instrument of half that worth as those your swords, made rich with the most noble blood of all this world.
Live a thousand years, I shall not find myself so apt to die; no place will please me so, no mean of death as here by Caesar, and by you cut off, the choice and master spirits of this age.
O Antony, beg not your death of us!
Though now we must appear bloody and cruel, as by our hands and this present act, you see we do, yet see you but our hands.
Our hearts you see not.

Your voice shall be as strong as any man's in the disposing of new dignities.

Only be patient till we have appeased the multitude, beside themselves with fear, and then we will deliver you the cause, why I, that did love Caesar when I struck him, have thus proceeded.

I doubt not of your wisdom.

Let each man render me his bloody hand. First, Marcus Brutus, will I shake with you...
Gentlemen all--
Alas, what shall I say? My credit now stands on such slippery ground that one of two bad ways you must conceit me, either a coward or a flatterer.
That I did love thee, Caesar, O, 'tis true!
If then thy spirit look upon us now, shall it not grieve thee dearer than thy death to see thy Antony making his peace, shaking the bloody fingers of thy foes...
Had I as many eyes as thou ast wounds, weeping as they stream forth thy blood, it ould become me better than close in terms of friendship with thine enemies.
Here wast thou bay'd, brave hart, here didst thou fall, and here thy hunters stand, sign'd in thy spoil, and crimson'd in thy lethe.
O world, thou wast the forest to this hart, and this, indeed, O world, the heart of thee. How like a deer strucken by many princes dost thou here lie!

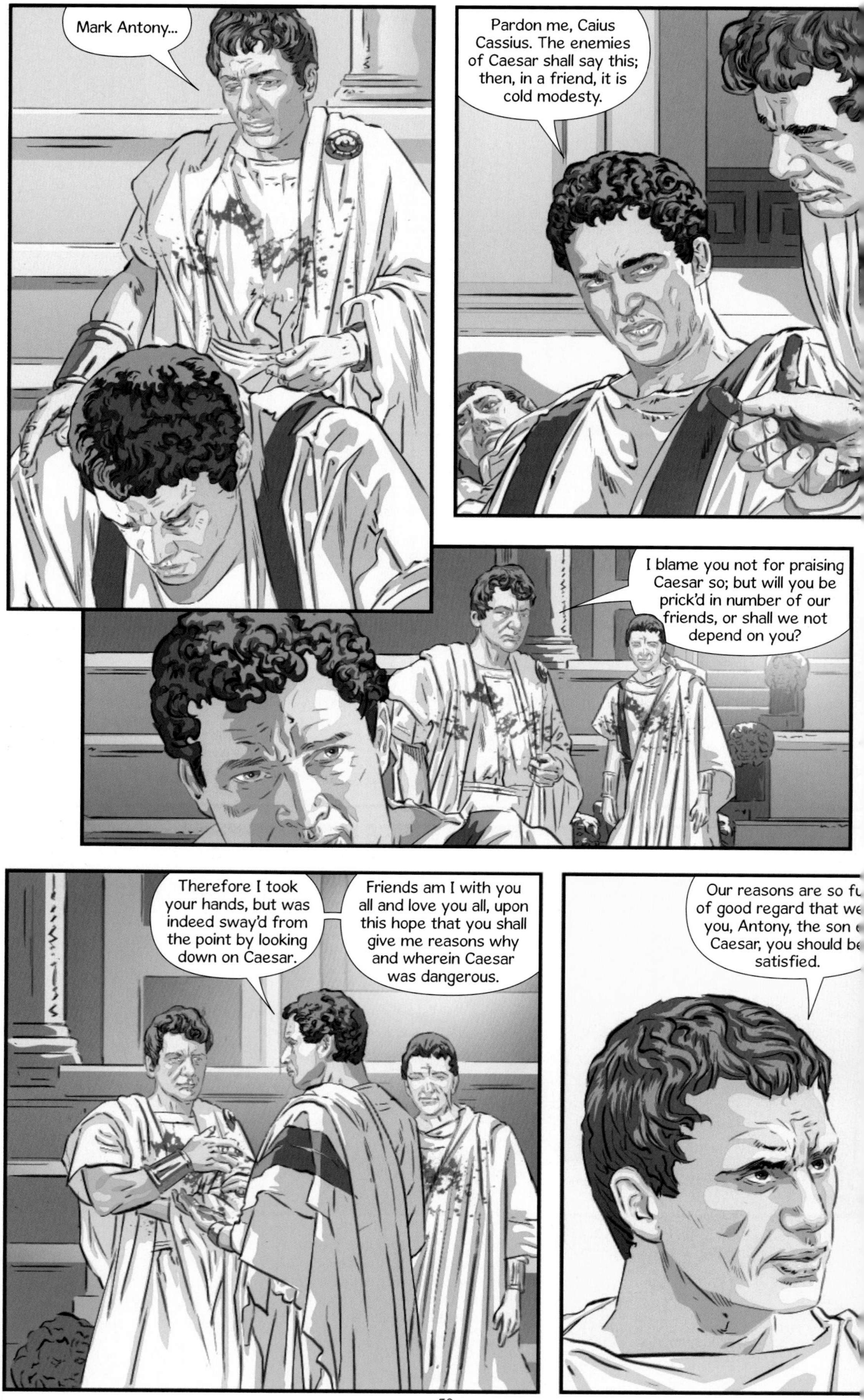

Mark Antony...

Pardon me, Caius Cassius. The enemies of Caesar shall say this; then, in a friend, it is cold modesty.

I blame you not for praising Caesar so; but will you be prick'd in number of our friends, or shall we not depend on you?

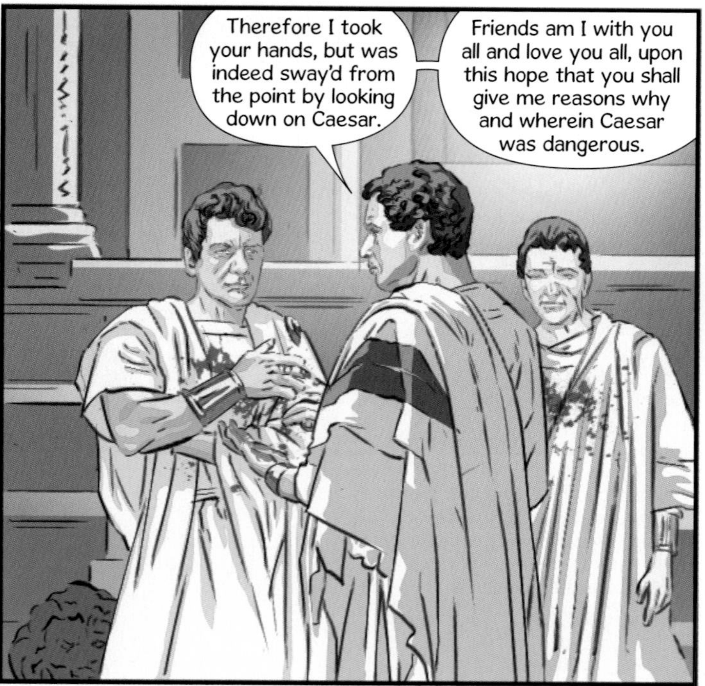

That's all I seek; and am moreover suitor that I may produce his body to the marketplace, and in the pulpit speak in the order of his funeral.
You shall, Mark Antony.
Brutus, a word with you...
You know not what you do. Do not consent that Antony speak in his funeral. Know you how much the people may be moved by that which he will utter?
I will myself into the pulpit first, and show the reason of our Caesar's death. What Antony shall speak, I will protest he speaks by leave and by permission..
It shall advantage more than do us wrong.
know not
at may fall;
like it not.

Mark Antony, here, take you Caesar's body.
You shall not in your funeral speech blame us, but speak all good you can devise of Caesar, and say you do't by our permission...
POMPEYS
Else shall you not have any hand at all about his funeral. And you shall speak in the same pulpit whereto I am going, after my speech is ended.
Be it so, I do desire no more.
Prepare the body then, and follow us.
O, pardon me, thou bleeding piece of earth, that I am meek and gentle with these butchers!

Thou art the ruins of the noblest man that ever lived in the tide of times. Woe to the hand that shed this costly blood! Over thy wounds now do I prophesy, which like dumb mouths do ope their ruby lips to beg the voice and utterance of my tongue.
POMPEYS
A curse shall light upon the limbs of men; domestic fury and fierce civil strife shall cumber all the parts of Italy.
Blood and destruction shall be so in use and dreadful objects so familiar that mothers shall but smile when they behold their infants quarter'd with the hands of war; all pity choked with custom of fell deeds...
...and Caesar's spirit ranging for revenge, with Ate* by his side, come hot from hell...
*Greek goddess of vengeance and menace
...shall in these confines with a monarch's voice cry 'Havoc!'
And let slip the dogs of war!

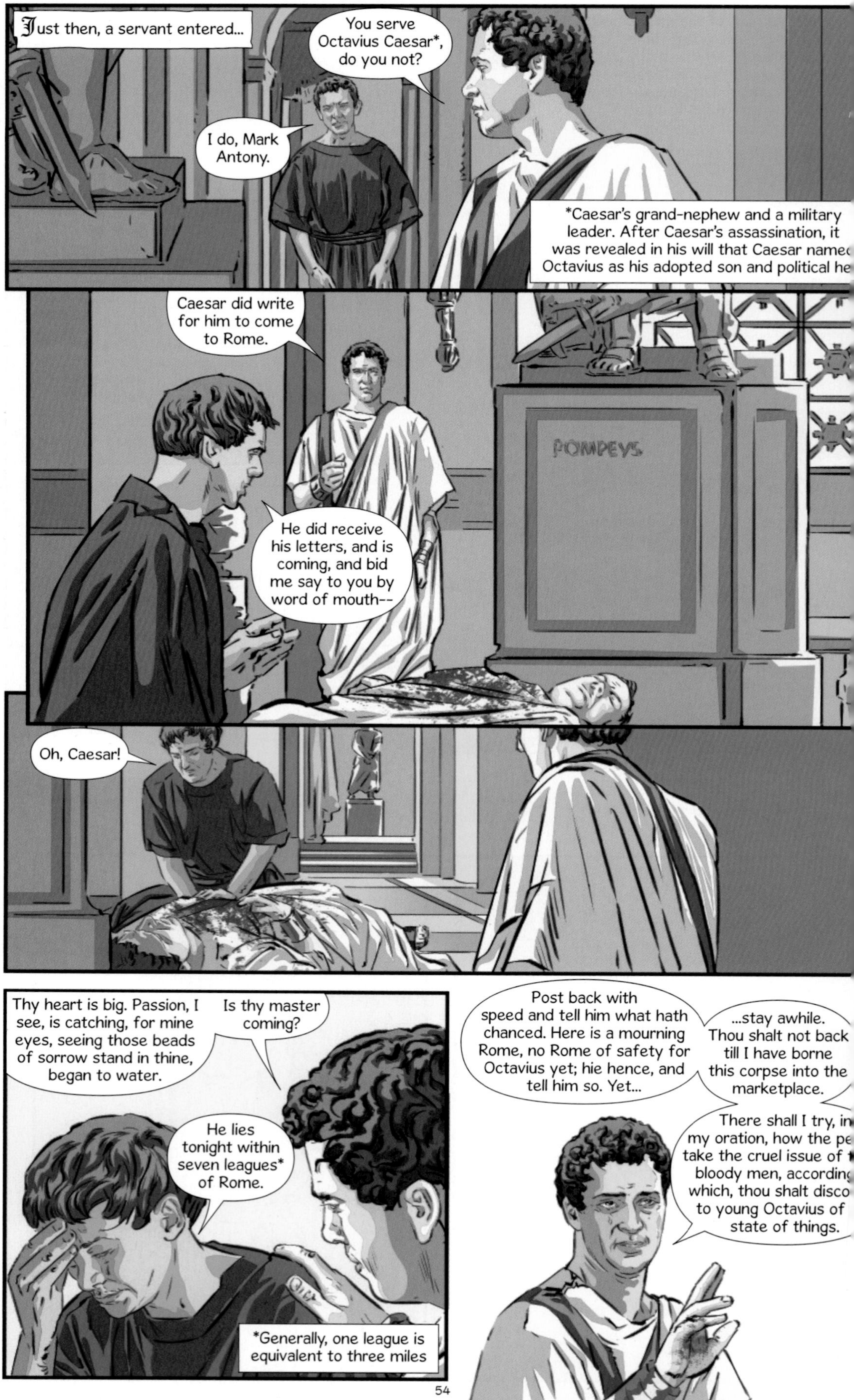

Just then, a servant entered...

You serve Octavius Caesar*, do you not?

I do, Mark Antony.

*Caesar's grand-nephew and a military leader. After Caesar's assassination, it was revealed in his will that Caesar name Octavius as his adopted son and political he

Caesar did write for him to come to Rome.

He did receive his letters, and is coming, and bid me say to you by word of mouth--

POMPEYS

Oh, Caesar!

Thy heart is big. Passion, I see, is catching, for mine eyes, seeing those beads of sorrow stand in thine, began to water.
Is thy master coming?
He lies tonight within seven leagues* of Rome.
*Generally, one league is equivalent to three miles

Post back with speed and tell him what hath chanced. Here is a mourning Rome, no Rome of safety for Octavius yet; hie hence, and tell him so. Yet...

...stay awhile. Thou shalt not back till I have borne this corpse into the marketplace.

There shall I try, in my oration, how the pe take the cruel issue of bloody men, accordin which, thou shalt disco to young Octavius of state of things.

ACT III, SCENE II
Outside the Senate, Brutus and Cassius faced the anger of the Roman people.
We will be satisfied! Let us be satisfied!
Then follow me and give me audience, friends. Those that will hear me speak, let 'em stay here; those that will follow Cassius, go with him.
Cassius, go you into the other street and part the numbers.
Romans, countrymen, and lovers! Hear me for my cause, and be silent, that you may hear.
Believe me for mine honor, and have respect to mine honor, that you may believe.
Censure me in your wisdom, and awake your senses, that you may the better judge.

If there be any in this assembly, any dear friend of Caesar's, to him I say that Brutus's love to Caesar was no less than his. If then that friend demand why Brutus rose against Caesar, this is my answer: not that I loved Caesar less...
...but that I loved Rome more.
Had you rather Caesar were living a die all slaves, than th Caesar were dead t live all freemen?
As Caesar loved me, I weep for him.
As he was fortunate, I rejoice at it.
As he was brave, I honor him.
But as he was ambitious, I slew him.
There is tears for his love.
Joy for his fortune.
Honor for his valor.
And death for his ambition.

ho is here so base that would be a bondman? Who is here so rude that would not be a Roman? If any, speak, for him have I offended.
Who is here so vile that will not love his country? If any, speak.

I pause for a reply.

Then none have I offended. I have done no more to aesar than you shall do to Brutus.
The question of his death is enrolled in the Capitol, his glory not xtenuated; nor his offenses enforced, for which he suffered death.

Here comes his body...

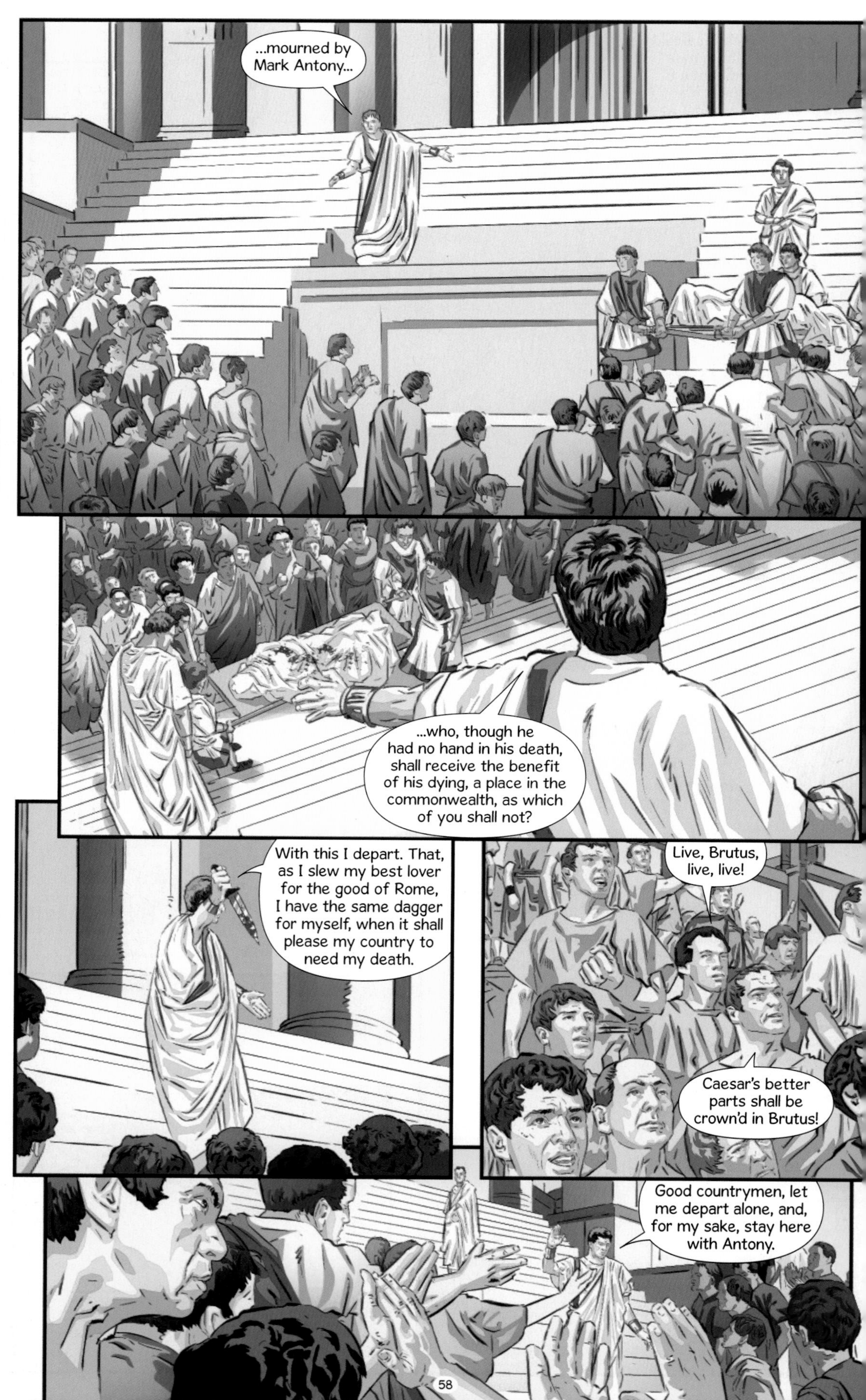
...mourned by Mark Antony...
...who, though he had no hand in his death, shall receive the benefit of his dying, a place in the commonwealth, as which of you shall not?
With this I depart. That, as I slew my best lover for the good of Rome, I have the same dagger for myself, when it shall please my country to need my death.
Live, Brutus, live, live!
Caesar's better parts shall be crown'd in Brutus!
Good countrymen, let me depart alone, and, for my sake, stay here with Antony.

Do grace to Caesar's corpse, and grace his speech tending to Caesar's glories, which Mark Antony, by our permission, is allow'd to make.
I do entreat you, not a man depart, save I alone, till Antony have spoke.
Stay, ho, and let us hear Mark Antony.
Let him go up into the public chair; we'll hear him. Noble Antony, go up!
For Brutus's sake, I am beholding to you.
What does he say of Brutus?
'Twere best he speak no harm of Brutus here!!
You gentle Romans...
Peace, ho! Let us hear him.

Friends, Romans, countrymen, lend me your ears!
I come to bury Caesar, not to praise him. The evil that men do lives after them, the good is oft interred with their bones. So let it be with Caesar.
The noble Brutus hath told you Caesar was ambitious; if it were so, it was a grievous fault, and grievously hath Caesar answer'd it.
Here, under leave of Brutus and the rest, for Brutus is an honorable man, so are they all, all honorable men, come I to speak in Caesar's funeral.
He was my friend, faithful and just to me.
But Brutus says he was ambitious.
And Brutus is an honorable man.

He hath brought many aptives home to Rome, vhose ransoms did the general coffers fill.
Did this in Caesar seem ambitious?
When that the poor have cried, Caesar hath wept; ambition should be made of sterner stuff.
Yet Brutus says he was ambitious.
And Brutus is an honorable man.
You all did see that on the Lupercal I thrice presented him a kingly crown, which he did thrice refuse.
Was this ambitious?
Yet Brutus says he was ambitious.
And sure he is an honorable man.
I speak not to disprove what Brutus spoke, but here I am to speak what I do know.
You all did love him once, not without cause; what cause withholds you then to mourn for him?
O Judgment, thou art fled to brutish beasts, and men have lost their reason!

Bear with me...
My heart is in the coffin there with Caesar, and I must pause till it come back to me.
Methinks there is much reason in his sayings.
If thou consider rightly of the matter, Caesar has had great wrong.
Mark'd ye his words? He would not take the crown; therefore 'tis certain he was not ambitious.
If it be found so, some will dear abide it!
Poor soul, his eyes are red as fire with weeping!
There's not a nobler man in Rome than Mark Antony.
Now mark him, he begins again to speak.

But yesterday the word of Caesar might have stood against the world. Now lies he there, and none so poor to do him reverence.
If I were disposed to stir your hearts and minds to mutiny and rage, I should do Brutus wrong and Cassius wrong, who, you all know, are honorable men.
I will not do them wrong.
I rather choose to wrong the dead, to wrong myself and you, than I will wrong such honorable men.
But here's a parchment with the seal of Caesar.
I found it in his closet; 'tis his will.
Let but the commons hear this testament – which, pardon me, I do not mean to read – and they would go and kiss dead Caesar's wounds and dip their napkins in his sacred blood, and, dying, mention it within their wills, bequeathing it as a rich legacy unto their issue.

We'll hear the will. Read it, Mark Antony.
The will! The will!
We will hear Caesar's will!

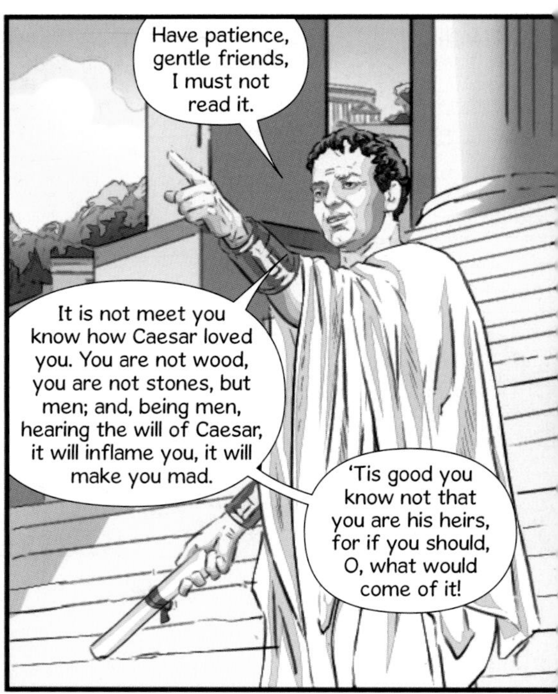
Have patience, gentle friends, I must not read it.
It is not meet you know how Caesar loved you. You are not wood, you are not stones, but men; and, being men, hearing the will of Caesar, it will inflame you, it will make you mad.
'Tis good you know not that you are his heirs, for if you should, O, what would come of it!

Read the will; we'll hear it, Antony. You shall read us the will, Caesar's will.

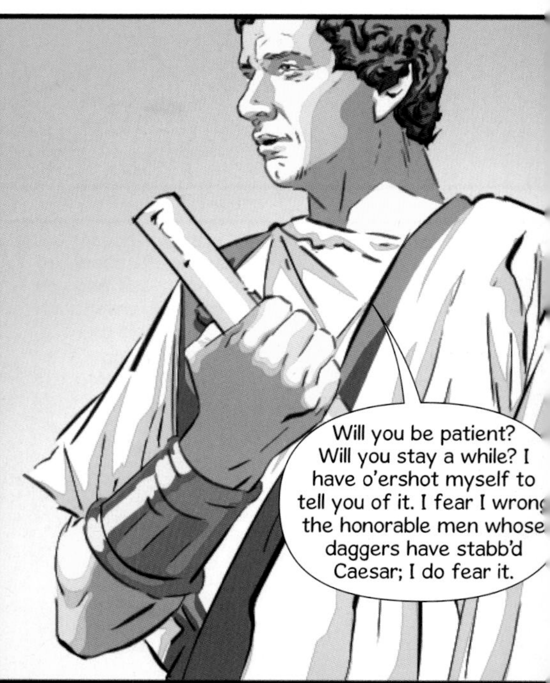
Will you be patient? Will you stay a while? I have o'ershot myself to tell you of it. I fear I wrong the honorable men whose daggers have stabb'd Caesar; I do fear it.

They were traitors. 'Honorable men!'
They were villains, murderers. The will! Read the will!
The will! The testament!

ou will compel
e then to read
the will?
Then make a ring about the corpse of Caesar, and let me show you him that made the will. Shall I descend? And will you give me leave?
Descend!
Room for Antony, most noble Antony!
Nay, press not so upon me, stand far off!
If you have tears, prepare to shed them now.
You all know this mantle. I remember the first time ever Caesar put it on; 'twas on a summer's evening, in his tent, that day he overcame the Nervii*.
*A Gallic tribe.
Look, in this place ran Cassius's dagger through...
See what a rent the envious Casca made...
Through this the well-beloved Brutus stabb'd; and as he pluck'd his cursed steel away, mark how the blood of Caesar follow'd it.
For Brutus, as you know, was Caesar's angel. Judge, O you gods, how dearly Caesar loved him!
This was the most unkindest cut of all.

For when the noble Caesar saw him stab, ingratitude, more strong than traitors' arms, quite vanquish'd him.
Then burst his mighty heart, and, in his mantle muffling up his face, even at the base of Pompey's statue, which all the while ran blood, great Caesar fell.
O, what a fall was there, my countrymen! Then I, and you, and all of us fell down, whilst bloody treason flourish'd over us.
O, now you weep, and I perceive you feel the dint of pity.
Kind souls, what weep you when you but behold our Caesar's vesture wounded? Look you here, here is himself, marr'd, as you see, with traitors.
O piteous spectacle!
O noble Caesar!
O traitors! Villains!
We will be revenged!
Revenge! About! Seek!
Burn! Kill!
Stay, countrymen.
Slay! Let not a traitor live!
Peace there! Hear the noble Antony!
We'll hear him, we'll follow him, we'll die with him.

Good friends, sweet friends, let me not stir you up to such a sudden flood of mutiny.
They that have done this deed are honorable. What private griefs they have, alas, I know not, that made them do it. They will, no doubt, with reasons answer you.
I come not, friends, to teal away your hearts. I n no orator, as Brutus is, ut, as you know me all, a lain blunt man, that love my friend.
For I have neither wit, nor words, nor worth, action, nor utterance, nor the power of speech, to stir men's blood.
I tell you that which you yourselves do know; show you sweet Caesar's wounds, poor poor dumb mouths, and bid them speak for me.
But were I Brutus, and Brutus Antony, there were an Antony would ruffle up your spirits and put a tongue in every wound of Caesar that should move the stones of Rome to rise and mutiny.
We will mutiny!
We'll burn the house of Brutus!
Away, then! Come, seek the conspirators!
Yet hear me, countrymen! Why, friends, you go to do you know not what. Wherein hath Caesar thus deserved your loves?
Alas, you know not; I must tell you then. You have forgot the will I told you of.

Here is the will, under Caesar's seal...
To every Roman citizen, he gives seventy-five drachmas*.
*Greek silver coins
Moreover, he hath left you all his walks, his private arbors, and new-planted orchards on this side Tiber; he hath left them you, and to your heirs for ever common pleasures, to walk abroad and recreate yourselves.
Here was a Caesar! Whe comes such another?
Never, never. Come, away, away! We'll burn his body in the holy place and with the brands fire the traitors' houses! Take up the body.
Go fetch fire!
Pluck down benches!
Pluck down forms, windows, anything!
Now let it work. Mischief, thou art afoot. Take thou what course thou wilt.
Sir, Octavius is already come to Rome. He and Lepidus are at Caesar's house.
And thither will I straight to visit him. He comes upon a wish. Fortune is merry, and in this mood, will give us anything.
I heard him say, Brutus and Cassius are rid like madmen through the gates of Rome.
Belike they had some notice of the people, how I had moved them. Bring me to Octavius.

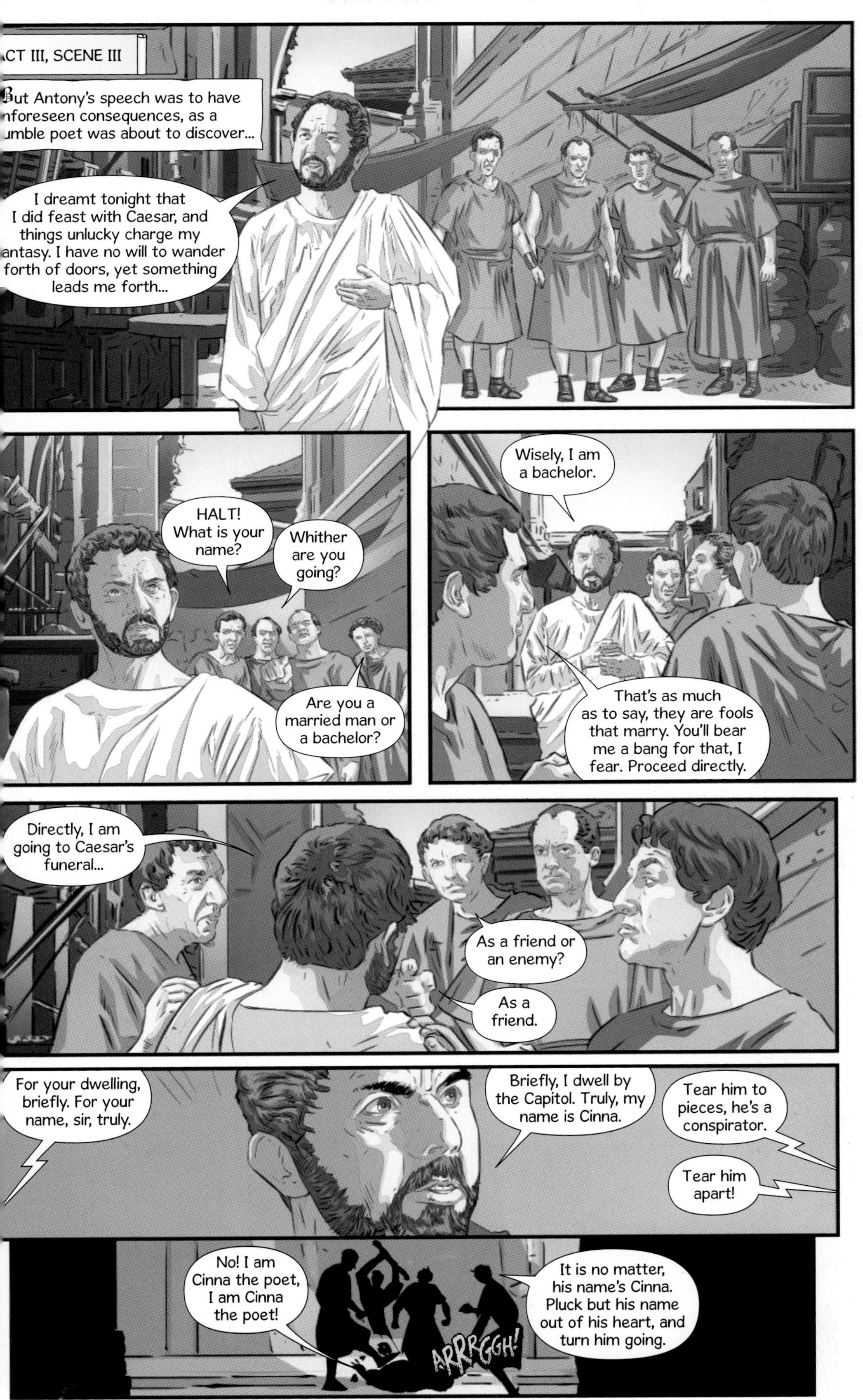

CT III, SCENE III
But Antony's speech was to have nforeseen consequences, as a umble poet was about to discover...
I dreamt tonight that I did feast with Caesar, and things unlucky charge my antasy. I have no will to wander forth of doors, yet something leads me forth...
HALT! What is your name?
Whither are you going?
Are you a married man or a bachelor?
Wisely, I am a bachelor.
That's as much as to say, they are fools that marry. You'll bear me a bang for that, I fear. Proceed directly.
Directly, I am going to Caesar's funeral...
As a friend or an enemy?
As a friend.
For your dwelling, briefly. For your name, sir, truly.
Briefly, I dwell by the Capitol. Truly, my name is Cinna.
Tear him to pieces, he's a conspirator.
Tear him apart!
No! I am Cinna the poet, I am Cinna the poet!
It is no matter, his name's Cinna. Pluck but his name out of his heart, and turn him going.
ARRRGGH!

ACT IV, SCENE I
Meanwhile, at his home, Mark Antony met with Caesar's deputy, Aemilius Lepidus, and Caesar's adopted son Gaius Octavius to draw up a list of rebels who should be killed or exiled to ensure Rome's peace, in the wake of Caesar's murder.
These many men then shall die; their names are checked on the list.
Your brother must die too. Do you consent, Lepidus?
I do consent on the condition that Publius shall not live, who is your nephew, Mark Antony.
He shall not live. Look, with a spot I damn him.
But, Lepidus, go you to Caesar's house, fetch the will hither, and we shall determine how to cut off some charge in legacies.
This is a slight unmeritable man, meet to be sent on errands. Is it fit, the three-fold world divided, he should stand one of the three to share it?
So you thought him, and took his voice who should be prickt to die in our black sentence and proscription.

Octavius, I have seen more days than you, and ugh we lay these honors on s man to ease ourselves of ivers slanderous loads, he hall but bear them as the ass bears gold...
...and having brought our treasure where we will, then take we down his load and turn him off to shake his ears and graze in commons.
You may do your will, but he's a tried and valiant soldier.
So is my horse, Octavius, and for that I do appoint him store of provender. It is a creature that I teach to fight, to wind, to stop, to run directly on, his corporal motion govern'd by my spirit. And, in some taste, is Lepidus but so.
And now, Octavius, listen great things. Brutus and Cassius are levying powers; we must straight make head; therefore let our alliance be combined, our best friends made, our best means stretcht out.
Let us do so, for we are bay'd about with many enemies; and some that smile have in their hearts, I fear, millions of mischiefs.

ACT IV, SCENE II
On the hills of Sardis, in the province of Lydia, Brutus had established a military camp, where he planned his revenge against Mark Antony.
But the strain of exile wore heavy on Caesar's killers, and Brutus feared that his alliance with Cassius was crumbling.
What now, Lucilius? Is Cassius near?
He is at hand; and Pindarus is come to do you salutation from his master.
He greets me well. Your master, Pindarus, in his own change, or by ill officers, hath given me some worthy cause to wish things done, undone. But, if he be at hand, I shall be satisfied.
I do not doubt but that my noble master will appear such as he is, full of regard and honor.
He is not doubted.
A word, Lucilius; how he received you, let me be resolved.
With courtesy and with respect enough, but not with such familiar instances, nor with such free and friendly conference, as he hath used of o
Thou hast described a hot friend cooling. Ever note, Lucilius, when love begins to sicken and decay it useth an enforced ceremony. There are no tricks in plain and simple faith...
...but hollow men, like horses hot at hand, make gallant show and promise of their mettle; but when they should endure the bloody spur, they fall their crests and like deceitful jades sink in the trial.

Comes his army on?

They mean this night in Sardis to be quarter'd; the greater part, the horse in general, are come with Cassius.

Hark, he is arrived. March gently on to meet him.

Most noble brother, you have done me wrong.

Judge me, you gods! Wrong I mine enemies? And, if not so, how should I wrong a brother?

Brutus, this sober form of yours hides wrongs, and when you do them--

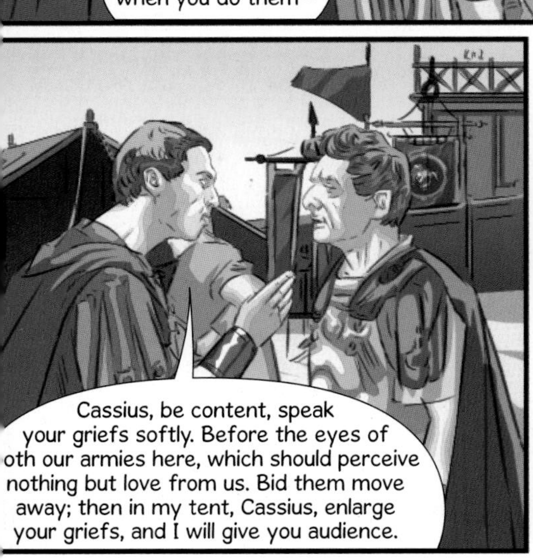

Cassius, be content, speak your griefs softly. Before the eyes of oth our armies here, which should perceive nothing but love from us. Bid them move away; then in my tent, Cassius, enlarge your griefs, and I will give you audience.

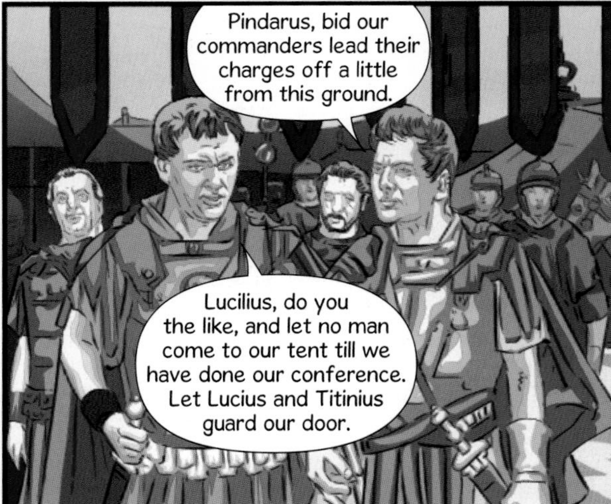

Pindarus, bid our commanders lead their charges off a little from this ground.
Lucilius, do you the like, and let no man come to our tent till we have done our conference. Let Lucius and Titinius guard our door.

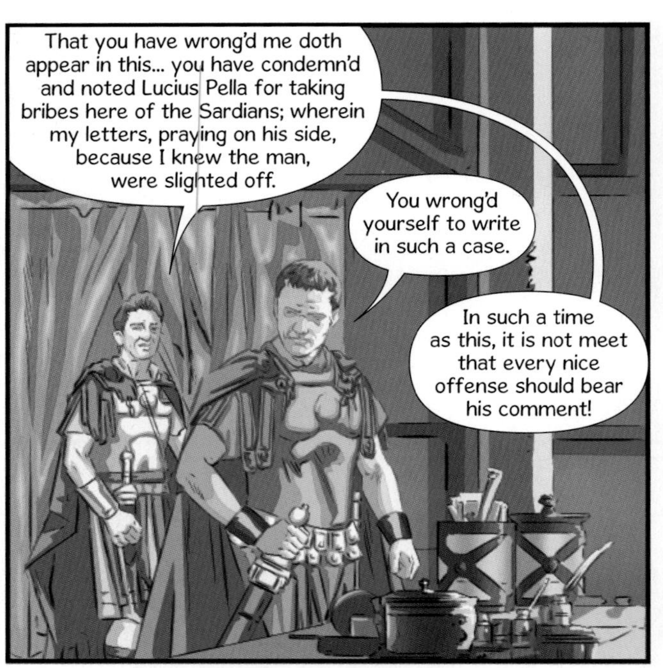
That you have wrong'd me doth appear in this... you have condemn'd and noted Lucius Pella for taking bribes here of the Sardians; wherein my letters, praying on his side, because I knew the man, were slighted off.
You wrong'd yourself to write in such a case.
In such a time as this, it is not meet that every nice offense should bear his comment!

Let me tell you, Cassius, you yourself are much condemn'd to have an itching palm, to sell and mart your offices for gold to undeservers.

I an itching palm? You know that you are Brutus that speaks this, or, by the gods, this speech were else your last!

The name of Cassius honors this corruption, and chastisement doth therefore hide his head.
Chastisement!
Remember March, the Ides of March remember. Did not great Julius bleed for justice's sake? What, shall one of us, that struck the foremost man of all this world but for supporting robbers, shall we now contaminate our fingers with base bribes?

Brutus, bay not me, I'll not endure it! You forget yourself, to hedge me in. I am a soldier; I, older in practice, abler than yourself to make conditions.
Go to! You are not, Cassius!

I am.
I say you are not.
Urge me no more, I shall forget myself!
Away, slight man!
Is't possible?
Hear me, for I will speak. Must I give way and room to your rash choler? Shall I be frighted when a madman stares?
O gods, ye gods! Must I endure all this?
All this? Ay, more!
et till your proud heart break! Go show your aves how choleric you are, and make your bondmen tremble.
Must I stand and crouch under your testy humor? By the gods, you shall digest the venom of your spleen, though it do split you, for, from this day forth, I'll use you for my mirth, yea, for my laughter, when you are waspish.
Is it come to this?
You say you are a better soldier. Let it appear so! Make your vaunting true, and it shall please me well.
You wrong me every way Brutus. I said, an elder soldier, not a better. Did I say 'better'?
If you did, I care not.
When Caesar lived, he durst not thus have moved me.
Peace, peace! You durst not so have tempted him!
Do not presume too much upon my love. I may do that I shall be sorry for.

You have done that you should be sorry for. There is no terror, Cassius, in your threats, for I am arm'd so strong in honesty, that they pass by me as the idle wind which I respect not.
I did send to you for certain sums of gold, which you denied me, for I can raise no money by vile means!

By heaven, I had rather coin my heart and drop my blood for drachmas than to wring from the hard hands of peasants, their vile trash by any indirection. I did send to you for gold to pay my legions, which you denied me.
When Marcus Brutus grows so covetous to lock such rascal counters from his friends, be ready, gods, with all your thunderbolts, dash him to pieces!
I denied you not.

You did.
I did not. He was but a fool that brought my answer back..
Brutus hath rived my heart. A friend should bear his friend's infirmities, but Brutus makes mine greater than they are.
I do not, till you practise them on me.

You love me not.
I do not like your faults.
A friendly eye could never see such faults.
A flatterer's would not, though they do appear as huge as high Olympus.

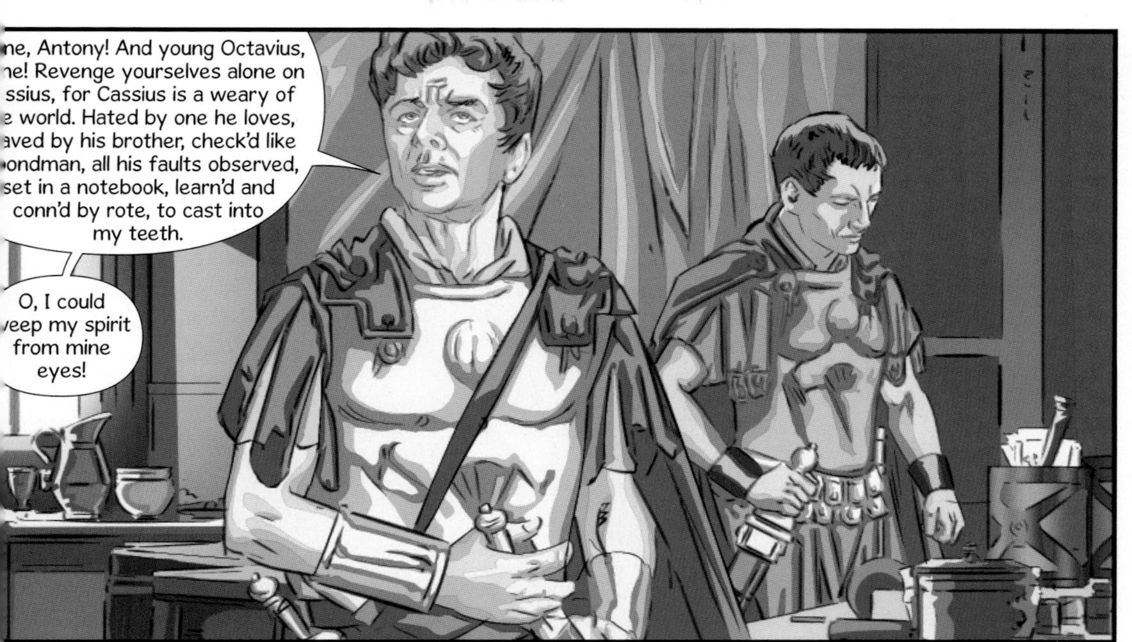

ne, Antony! And young Octavius, ne! Revenge yourselves alone on ssius, for Cassius is a weary of e world. Hated by one he loves, aved by his brother, check'd like ondman, all his faults observed, set in a notebook, learn'd and conn'd by rote, to cast into my teeth.
O, I could veep my spirit from mine eyes!

There is my dagger, and here my naked breast; within, a heart dearer than Pluto's* mine, richer than gold.
Strike, as thou didst at Caesar, for I know, when thou didst hate him worst, thou lovedst him better than ever thou lovedst Cassius.

*The Roman god of wealth and the Underworld

Sheathe your dagger. Be angry when you will, it shall have scope. Do what you will, dishonor shall be humor.

O Cassius, you are yoked with a lamb that carries anger as the flint bears fire, who, much enforced, shows a hasty spark, and straight is cold again.

Hath Cassius lived to be but mirth and laughter to his Brutus, when grief and blood ill-temper'd vexeth him?

When I spoke that, I was ill-temper'd too.

Do you confess so much? Give me your hand.

And my heart too.

O Brutus! Have not you love enough to bear with me, when that rash humor which my mother gave me makes me forgetful?

Yes, Cassius, and from henceforth, when you are over-earnest with your Brutus, he'll think your mother chides, and leave you so.

Suddenly, a wild-eyed poet burst into the tent...
You shall not come to them!
Nothing but death shall stay me!
How now, what's the matter?

For shame, you generals! What do you mean? Love and be friends, as two such men should be. For I have seen more years, I'm sure, than ye.

Ha, ha! How vilely doth this cynic rhyme!
Get you hence, sirrah! Saucy fellow, hence!
Bear with him, Brutus, 'tis his fashion..
I'll know his humor when he knows his time. What should the wars do with these jigging fools? Companion, hence!

Lucilius and Titinius, bid the commanders prepare to lodge their companies tonight.
And come yourselves, and bring Messala with you immediately to us.

Lucius, a bowl of wine!

I did not hink you could have been so angry.
O Cassius, I am sick of many griefs.

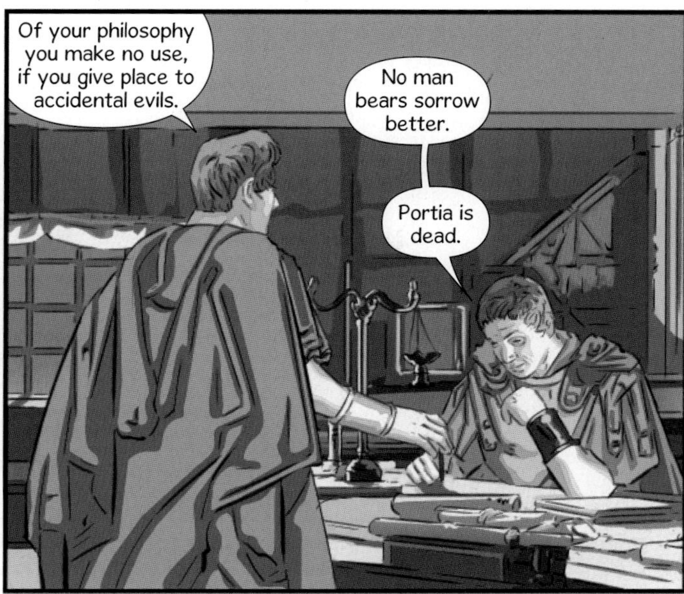

Of your philosophy you make no use, if you give place to accidental evils.
No man bears sorrow better.
Portia is dead.

Ha? Portia?

She is dead.

w escaped I killing n I cross'd you so? nsupportable and uching loss! Upon what sickness?

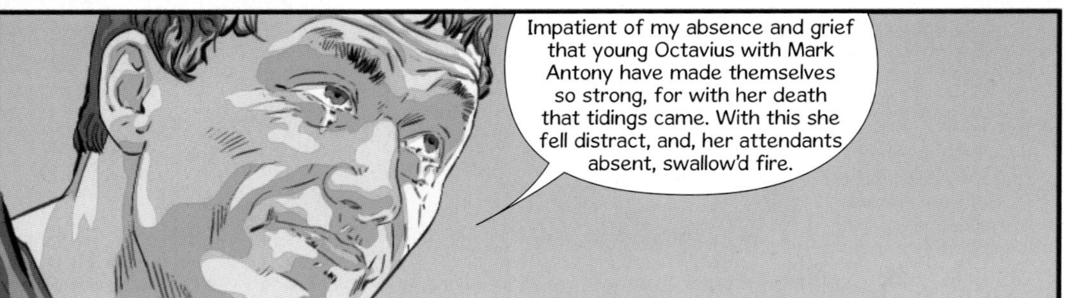

Impatient of my absence and grief that young Octavius with Mark Antony have made themselves so strong, for with her death that tidings came. With this she fell distract, and, her attendants absent, swallow'd fire.

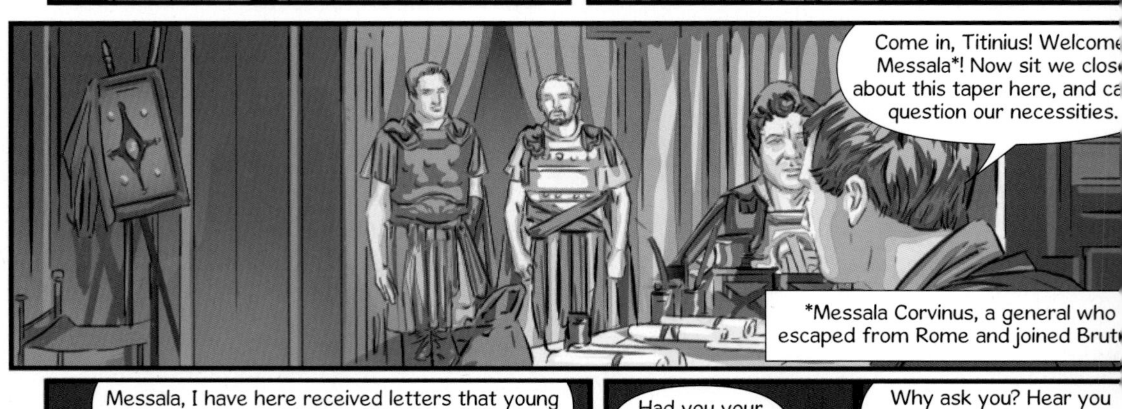

*Messala Corvinus, a general who escaped from Rome and joined Brut

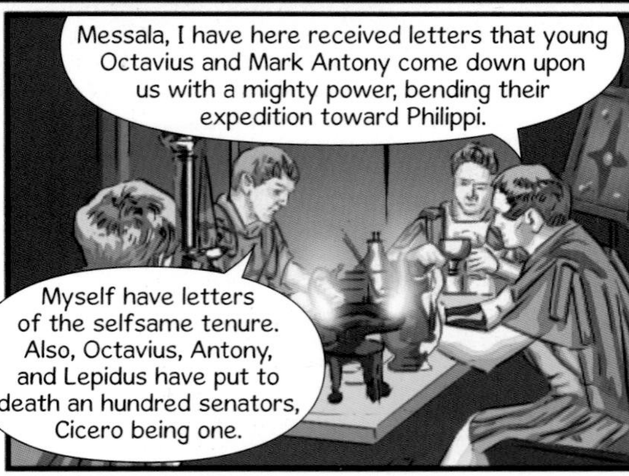

Why, farewell, Portia.
We must die, Messala. With meditating that she must die once, I have the patience to endure it now.

Even so great men great losses should endure.

I have as much of this in art as you, but yet my nature could not bear it so.
Well, to our work alive.

What do you think of marching to Philippi presently?
I do not think it good. 'Tis better that the enemy seek us; so shall he waste his means, weary his soldiers, doing himself offense, whilst we lying still are full of rest, defense, and nimbleness.

Good reasons must, of force, give place to better.
The people 'twixt Philippi and this ground do stand but in a forced affection, for they have grudged us contribution. The enemy, marching along by them, by them shall make a fuller number up, from which advantage shall we cut him off if at Philippi we do face him there, these people at our back.

Hear me, brother.
Under your pardon. You must note beside that our legions are brimful, our cause is ripe. The enemy increaseth every day; we, at the height, are ready to decline.
There is a tide in the affairs of men which taken at the flood leads on to fortune. Omitte all the voyage of their life is boun in shallows and in miseries.

Then, with your will, go on. We'll along ourselves and meet them at Philippi.
The deep of night is crept upon our talk, and nature must obey necessity, which we will niggard with a little rest. There is no more to say?
No more. Good night. Early tomorrow will we rise and hence.
Farewell, good Messala! Good night, Titinius!

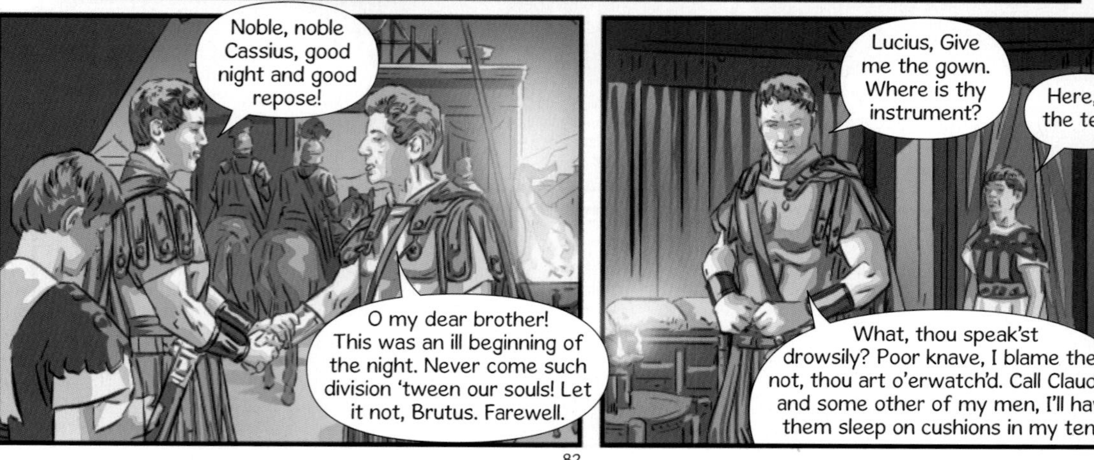
Noble, noble Cassius, good night and good repose!
O my dear brother! This was an ill beginning of the night. Never come such division 'tween our souls! Let it not, Brutus. Farewell.
Lucius, Give me the gown. Where is thy instrument?
Here, i the ten
What, thou speak'st drowsily? Poor knave, I blame thee not, thou art o'erwatch'd. Call Claudiu and some other of my men, I'll have them sleep on cushions in my tent.

Calls my lord?
I pray you, sirs, lie in my tent and sleep. It may be I shall raise you by and by on business to my brother Cassius.
So please you, we will stand and watch your pleasure.
I will not have it so. Lie down, good sirs.
Lucius, canst thou hold up thy heavy eyes a while, and touch thy instrument a strain or two?
Ay, my lord, an't please you.
It does, my boy. I trouble thee too much, but thou art willing.
It is my duty, sir.
I should not urge thy duty past thy might; I know young bloods look for a time of rest.
O murderous slumber, layest thou thy leaden mace upon my boy that plays thee music. Gentle knave, good night. I will not do thee so much wrong to wake thee. If thou dost nod, thou break'st thy instrument; I'll take it from thee. And, good boy, good night.
Let me see, let me see... How ill this taper burns!

Ha, who comes here?
I think it is the weakness of mine eyes that shapes this monstrous apparition. Art thou some god, some angel, or some devil that makest my blood cold, and my hair to stare?
Speak to me what thou art!
Thy evil spirit, Brutus.
Why comest thou?
To tell thee thou shalt see me at Philippi.
Well, then I shall see thee again?
Ay, at Philippi.
Why, I will see thee at Philippi then.
Now I have taken heart thou vanishest. Ill spirit, I would hold more talk with thee.
Boy, Lucius! Varro! Claudius! Sirs, awake! Claudius!
Didst thou see anything?
Nothing, my lord.
Nor I, my lord.
Go and commend me to my brother Cassius. Bid him set on his powers betimes before, and we will follow.
It shall be done, my lord.

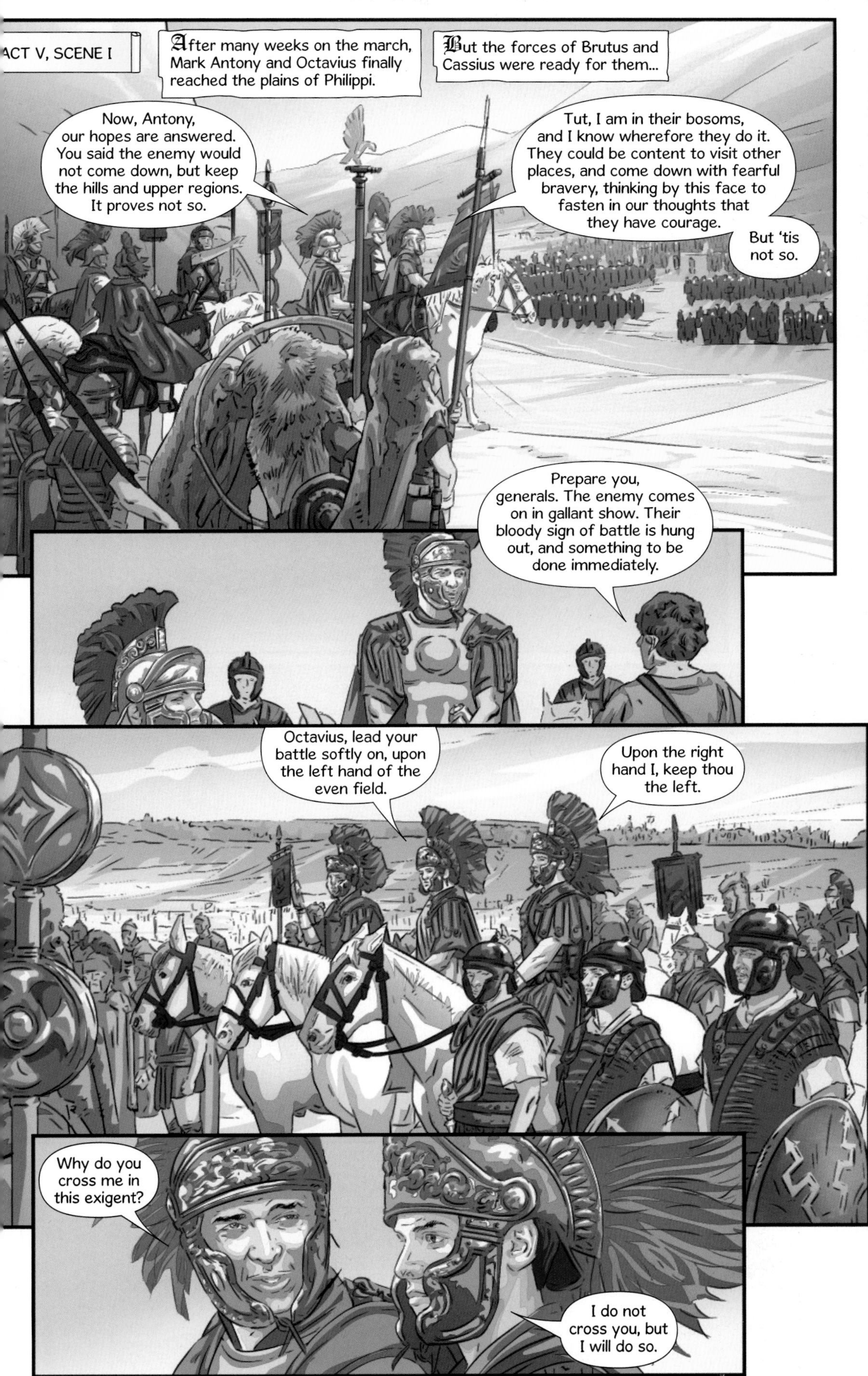
ACT V, SCENE I
After many weeks on the march, Mark Antony and Octavius finally reached the plains of Philippi.
But the forces of Brutus and Cassius were ready for them...
Now, Antony, our hopes are answered. You said the enemy would not come down, but keep the hills and upper regions. It proves not so.
Tut, I am in their bosoms, and I know wherefore they do it. They could be content to visit other places, and come down with fearful bravery, thinking by this face to fasten in our thoughts that they have courage.
But 'tis not so.
Prepare you, generals. The enemy comes on in gallant show. Their bloody sign of battle is hung out, and something to be done immediately.
Octavius, lead your battle softly on, upon the left hand of the even field.
Upon the right hand I, keep thou the left.
Why do you cross me in this exigent?
I do not cross you, but I will do so.

They stand, and would have parley.
Stand fast, Titinius. We must out and talk.

Mark Antony, shall we give sign of battle?
No, Caesar, we will answer on their charge.
Make forth, the generals would have some words.

Stir not until the signal.

Words before blows. Is it so, countrymen?
Not that we love words better, as you do.
Good words are better than bad strokes, Octavius.
In your bad strokes, Brutus, you give good words. Witness the hole you made in Caesar's heart, crying 'Long live! Hail, Caesar!'

Antony, the posture of your blows are yet unknown. But for your words, they rob the Hybla bees, and leave them honeyless.
Not stingless too?
O, yes, and soundless too, for you have stol'n their buzzing, Antony, and very wisely threat before you sting.

Villains! You did not so when you show'd your teeth like apes, and fawn'd like hounds, and bow'd like bondmen kissing Caesar's feet, whilst damned Casca, like a cur, behind struck Caesar on the neck. O you flatterers!

Flatterers? Now, Brutus, thank yourself. This tongue had not offended so today if Cassius might have ruled.

Come, come, the cause. If arguing make us sweat, the proof of it will turn to redder drops.
Look, I draw a sword against conspirators. When think you that the sword goes up again? Never, till Caesar's three and thirty wounds be well avenged, or till another Caesar have added slaughter to the sword of traitors.

Caesar, thou canst not die by traitors' hands, unless thou bring'st them with thee.

So I hope! I was not born to die on Brutus's sword.
O, if thou wert the noblest of thy strain, young man, thou couldst not die more honorable.

A peevish school boy, worthless of such honor, join'd with a masker and a reveller!

Old Cassius still!

Com
Anton
awa

Defiance, traitors, hurl we in your teeth. If you dare fight today, come to the field. If not, when you have stomachs.

Why, now, blow wind, swell billow, and swim bark! The storm is up, and all is on the hazard!

Ho, Lucilius! Hark, a word with you.
My lord?
Messala!
What says my general?
Messala, this is my birthday. Give me thy hand, Messala. Be thou my witness that, against my will, as Pompey was, am I compell'd to set upon one battle all our liberties.
You know that I held Epicurus* strong, and his opinion. Now I change my mind...
*An ancient Greek philosopher whose teachings played an important role in the development of science and scientific method.
Coming from Sardis, on our former ensign, two mighty eagles fell, and there they perch'd, gorging and feeding from our soldiers' hands, who to Philippi here consorted us.
This morning are they fled away and gone, and in their steads do ravens, crows, and kites fly o'er our heads and downward look on us, as we were sickly prey.
Their shadows seem a canopy most fatal, under which our army lies, ready to give up the ghost.
Believe not so.

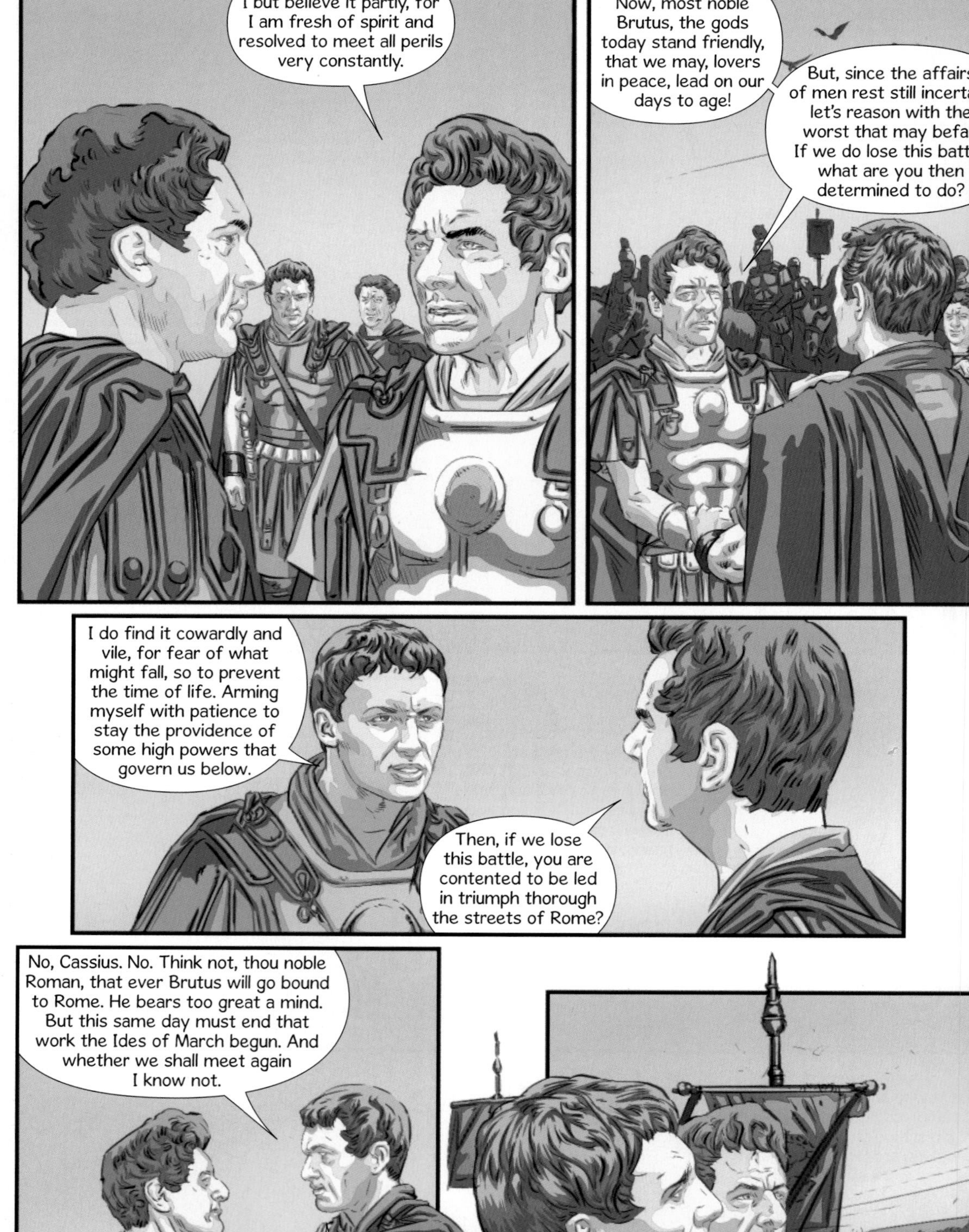
I but believe it partly, for I am fresh of spirit and resolved to meet all perils very constantly.
Now, most noble Brutus, the gods today stand friendly, that we may, lovers in peace, lead on our days to age!
But, since the affairs of men rest still incerta let's reason with the worst that may befal If we do lose this batt what are you then determined to do?
I do find it cowardly and vile, for fear of what might fall, so to prevent the time of life. Arming myself with patience to stay the providence of some high powers that govern us below.
Then, if we lose this battle, you are contented to be led in triumph thorough the streets of Rome?
No, Cassius. No. Think not, thou noble Roman, that ever Brutus will go bound to Rome. He bears too great a mind. But this same day must end that work the Ides of March begun. And whether we shall meet again I know not.
Therefore our everlasting farewell take. For ever, and for ever, farewell, Cassius! If we do meet again, why, we shall smile.
For ever and for ever farewell, Brutus! If we do meet again, we'll smile indeed.
Why then, lead on. O, that a man might know the end of this day's business ere it come! But it sufficeth that the day will end, and then the end is known.
Come, h Away!

ACT V, SCENE II

As horns sounded across the plains of Philippi, the battle began. History was to remain witness to how the fate of Rome itself would be decided on those bloody fields.

The air rang with the clash of swords as the two armies fought to the last.

The tides of the battle kept changing, and at one point of time it seemed Octavius's legion would fail to put up the fight.

LEG VI VERRARA

Ride, ride, Messala, ride, and give these bills unto the legions on the other side.

Let them set on at once, for I perceive but cold demeanor in Octavius's wing, and sudden push gives them the overthrow.

Ride! Ride, Messala! Let them all come down!

ACT V, SCENE III

While Brutus's army put up a valiant fight and gave the enemies a flutter, i was a different story in Cassius's cam

O, look, Titinius, look, the villains fly!

Myself have to mine own turn'd enemy. This ensign here of mine was turning back; I slew the coward, and did take it from him.

O Cassius, Brutus gave the word too early...

...who, having some advantage on Octavius, took it too eagerly. His soldiers fell to spoil, whilst we by Antony are all enclosed.

Fly further off, my lord, fly further off!
Mark Antony is in your tents, my lord! Fly, therefore, noble Cassius, fly far off!

This hill is far enough...
Look, look, Titinius! Are those my tents where I perceive the fire?
They are, my lord.

inius, mount thou my horse and de thy spurs in him till he have ought thee up to yonder troops nd here again, that I may rest assured whether yond troops are friend or enemy.
I will be here again, even with a thought.
Go, Pindarus, get higher on that hill. My sight was ever thick; regard Titinius, and tell me what thou notest about the field.
This day I breathed first... time is come round, and where I did begin, there shall I end...
...my life is run his compass.
Sirrah, what news?
Titinius is enclosed round about with horsemen that make to him on the spur; yet he spurs on. Now they are almost on him.
Now Titinius! Now some light...
O, he lights too. He's ta'en!
And, hark! They shout for joy!
HURRAH!

Come down. Behold no more.
O, coward that I am to live so long to see my best friend ta'en before my face!

So, I am free. Yet would not so have been, durst I have done my will. O Cassius! Far from this country Pindarus shall run where never Roman shall take note of him.

It is but change, Titinius, for Octavius is overthrown by noble Brutus's power, as Cassius's legions are by Antony.
These tidings would well comfort Cassius.

Is not that he that lies upon the ground?
He lies not like the living. O my heart!
Cassius is no more. O setting sun, as in thy d rays thou dost sink to ight, so in his red blood Cassius's day is set, the sun of Rome is set!
Our day is gone! Our deeds are done! Mistrust of my success hath done this deed.
Mistrust of good uccess hath done this deed. O hateful error, melancholy's hild! Why dost thou show to he apt thoughts of men the things that are not?

What, Pindarus! Where art thou, Pindarus?
Seek him, Titinius, whilst I go to meet the noble Brutus, thrusting this report into his ears. I may say 'thrusting' it, for piercing steel and darts envenomed shall be as welcome to the ears of Brutus as tidings of this sight.

Hie you, Messala, and I will seek for Pindarus the while.

Why didst thou send me forth, brave Cassius? Did I not meet thy friends? And did not they put on my brows this wreath of victory, and bid me give it thee? Didst thou not hear their shouts?

Alas, thou hast misconstrued everything!

But, hold thee, take this garland on thy brow. Thy Brutus bid me give it thee, and I will do his bidding. Brutus, come apace, and see how I regarded Caius Cassius.

By your leave, gods, this is a Roman's part...

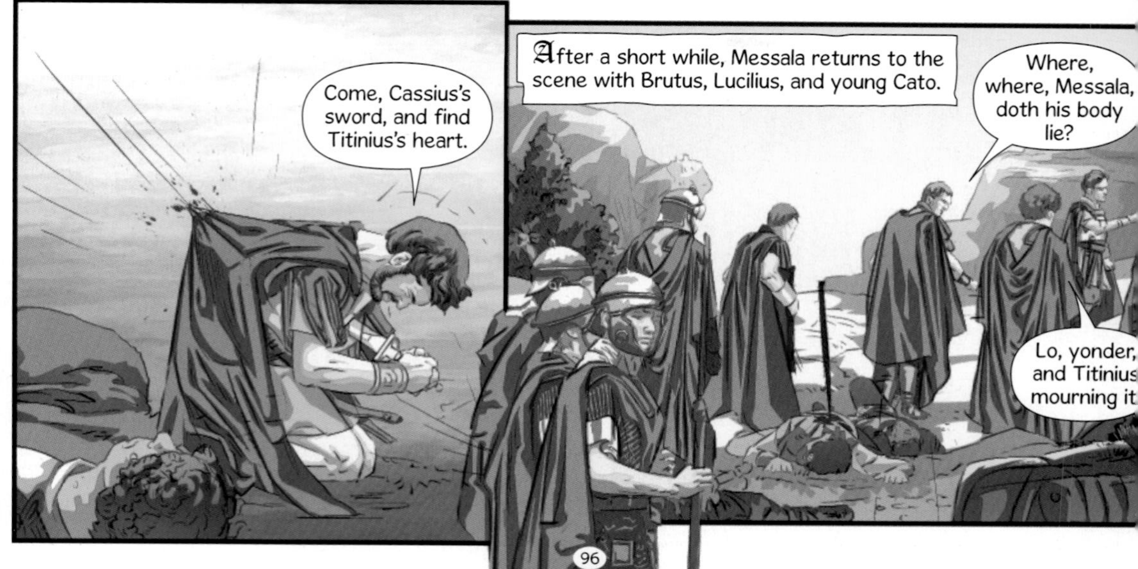

Come, Cassius's sword, and find Titinius's heart.
After a short while, Messala returns to the scene with Brutus, Lucilius, and young Cato.
Where, where, Messala, doth his body lie?
Lo, yonder, and Titinius mourning it

Oh Titinius!
He is slain!

O Julius Caesar, thou art mighty yet! Thy spirit walks abroad, and turns our swords in our own proper entrails.

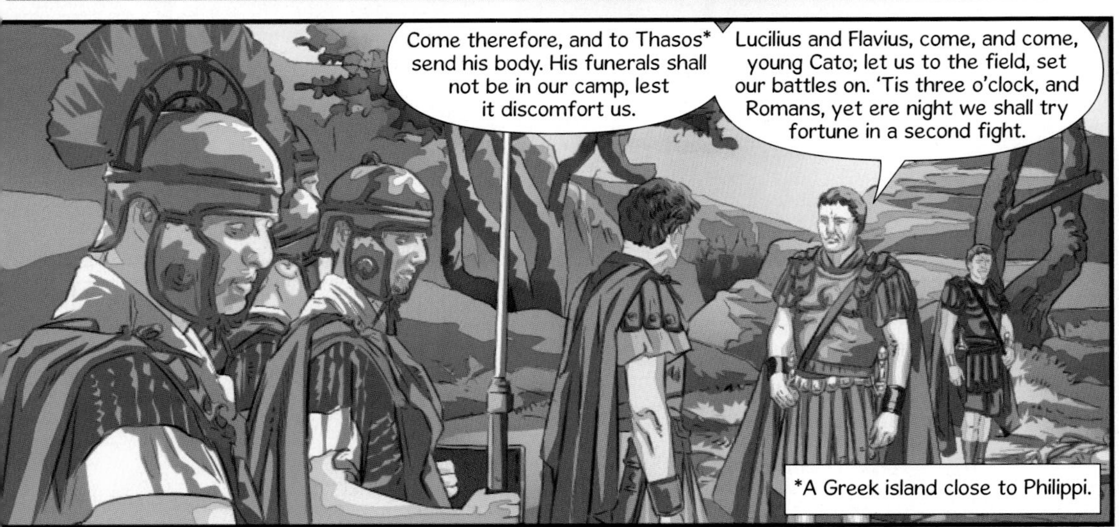

*A Greek island close to Philippi.

ACT V, SCENE IV

ly I yield to die. ere is so much thou wilt kill me aight. Here, I will y you to kill me right now!
Kill Brutus, and be honor'd in his death.

We must not. A noble prisoner!
Room, ho! Tell Antony, Brutus is ta'en.

Brutus is ta'en, Brutus is ta'en, my lord!
Where is he?

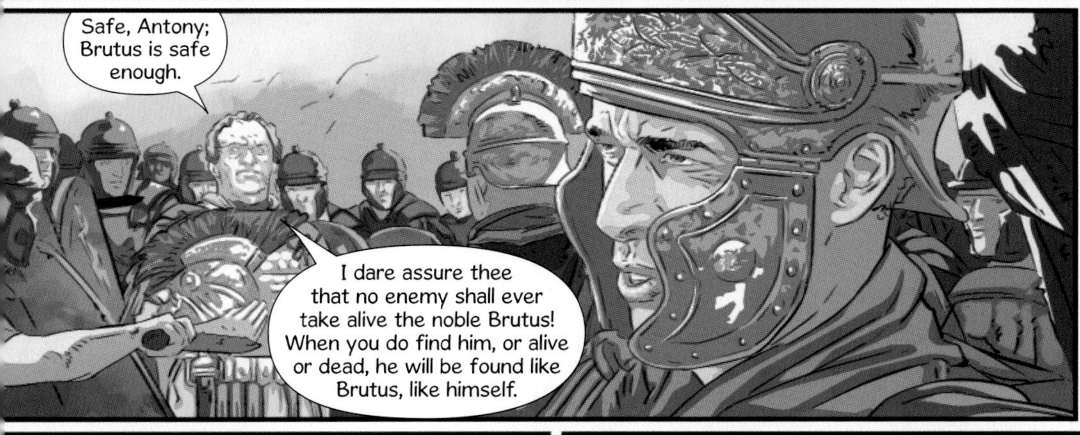
Safe, Antony; Brutus is safe enough.
I dare assure thee that no enemy shall ever take alive the noble Brutus! When you do find him, or alive or dead, he will be found like Brutus, like himself.

This is not Brutus, friend, but I assure you a prize no less in worth.
Keep this man fe, give him all kindness; I had rather have such men my friends than enemies.

Go on, and see whether Brutus be alive or dead. And bring us word unto Octavius's tent how everything is chanced.

ACT V, SCENE V

As the day drew to a close, Brutus was forced to admit defeat. His forces were slaughtered and his friends either slain or taken prisoner.

Come, poor remains of friends, rest on this rock.

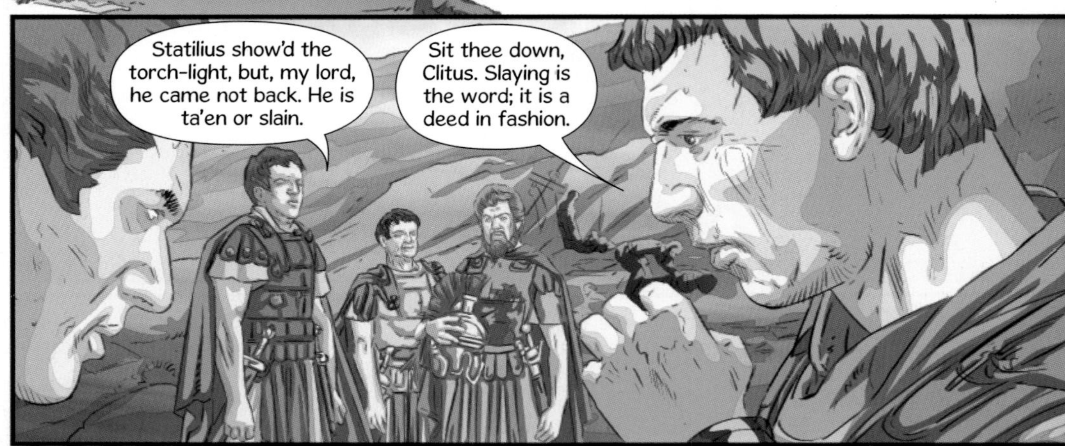

Statilius show'd the torch-light, but, my lord, he came not back. He is ta'en or slain.
Sit thee down, Clitus. Slaying is the word; it is a deed in fashion.

Hark, Clitus...
[whisper]
What! I, my lord?!
No, not for all the world! I'll rather kill myself!

Peace then, no words.

Hark thee, Dardanius...
[whisper]
Shall I do such a deed?

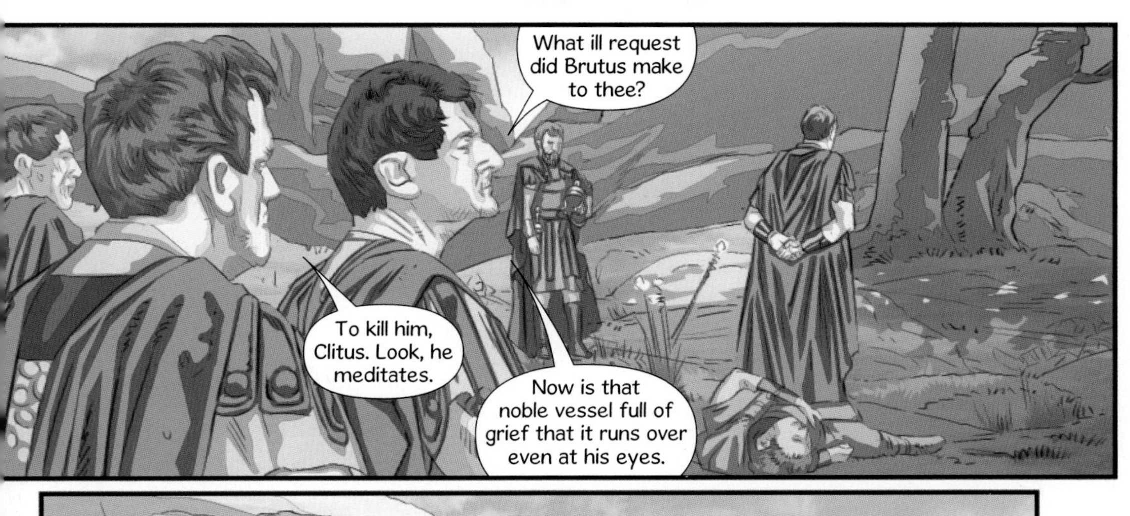
What ill request did Brutus make to thee?
To kill him, Clitus. Look, he meditates.
Now is that noble vessel full of grief that it runs over even at his eyes.

Come hither, good Volumnius, list a word.
What says my lord?

I know my hour is come.
Not so, my lord...

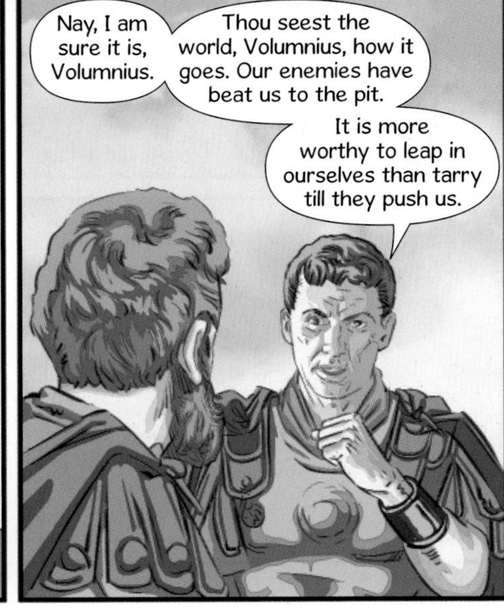
Nay, I am sure it is, Volumnius.
Thou seest the world, Volumnius, how it goes. Our enemies have beat us to the pit.
It is more worthy to leap in ourselves than tarry till they push us.

Good Volumnius, thou know'st that we two went to school together. Even for that our love of old, I prithee, hold thou my sword-hilts, whilst I run on it.
That's not an office for a friend, my lord.

Fly, fly, my lord, there is no tarrying here!

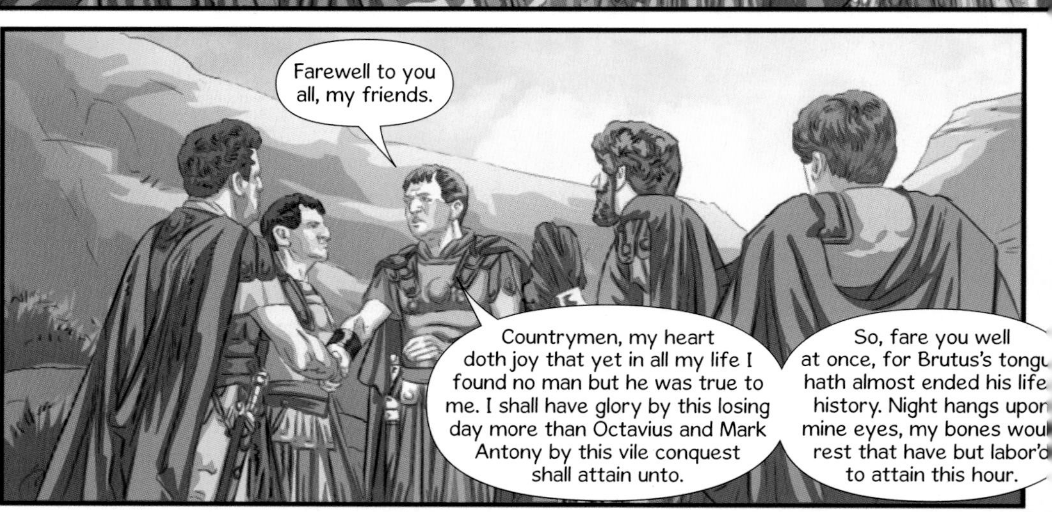
Farewell to you all, my friends.
Countrymen, my heart doth joy that yet in all my life I found no man but he was true to me. I shall have glory by this losing day more than Octavius and Mark Antony by this vile conquest shall attain unto.
So, fare you well at once, for Brutus's tongu hath almost ended his life history. Night hangs upon mine eyes, my bones woul rest that have but labor'd to attain this hour.

Fly, my lord, fly.
Hence! I will follow.

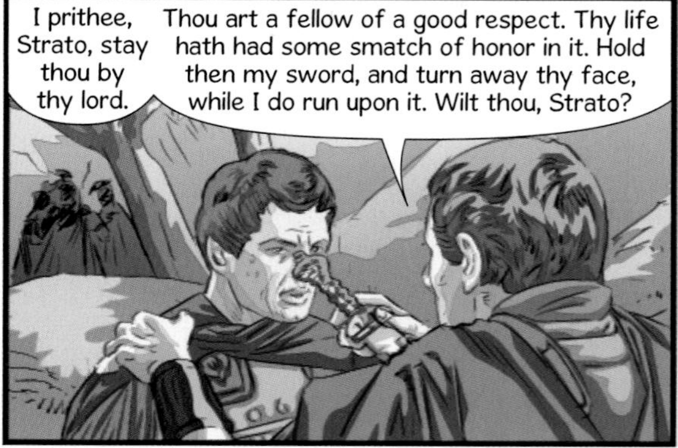
I prithee, Strato, stay thou by thy lord.
Thou art a fellow of a good respect. Thy life hath had some smatch of honor in it. Hold then my sword, and turn away thy face, while I do run upon it. Wilt thou, Strato?

Give me your hand first. Fare you well, my lord.
Farewell, good Strat

Caesar, now be still...
I kill'd not thee with half so good a will.
Mark Antony and Octavius arrived at the scene too late...
What man is that?
My master's man.
Strato, where is your master?

Free from the bondage you are in, Messala. The conquerors can but make a fire of him, for Brutus only overcame himself.
And no man else hath honor by his death.
So Brutus should be found. I thank thee, Brutus, that thou hast proved Lucilius's saying true.

All that served Brutus, I will entertain them. Strato, wilt thou bestow thy time with me?

Ay, if Messala will prefer me to you.

Do so, good Messala.

How died my master, Strato?

I held the sword, and he did run on it.

Octavius, then take him to follow thee that did the latest service to my master.

This was the noblest Roman of them all.
All the conspirators, save only he, did that they did in envy of great Caesar.
He only, in a general honest thought and common good to all, made one of them. His life was gentle, and the elements so mixt in him that Nature might stand up and say to all the world, 'This was a man!'

According to his virtue let us use him with all respect and rites of burial. Within my tent his bones tonight shall lie, most like a soldier, order'd honorably.

Call the field to rest, and let's away to part the glories of this happy day.

After the Curtain Fell

So, what happened to the characters in Julius Caesar after the end of the play? Let's find out...

Mark Antony

He shared the rule of Rome for a while with Octavius and Lepidus. He fell out with Octavius and the country was plunged into civil war, which ended with Mark Antony's defeat at Alexandria. Rather than submit to Octavius, Mark Antony and his lover Queen Cleopatra committed suicide.

Octavius

After defeating his old ally Mark Antony in a bid for power, Octavius became the unrivaled ruler of Rome. He was the founder of the Roman Empire and after changing his name to Augustus Caesar, he became first in a long line of Roman Emperors. He died aged 75 in 14 A.D.

Lepidus

Marcus Lepidus joined Octavius and Mark Antony in sharing the rule of Rome. He took control of Rome's western provinces. However, Octavius thought him too close to Mark Antony and accused him of attempted rebellion. He was removed from office and sent into exile. He died peacefully in 13 B.C.

The Show Must Go On

Shakespeare's *Julius Caesar* has a long and illustrious past. Let's take a look at some of the most notable stories related to the play!

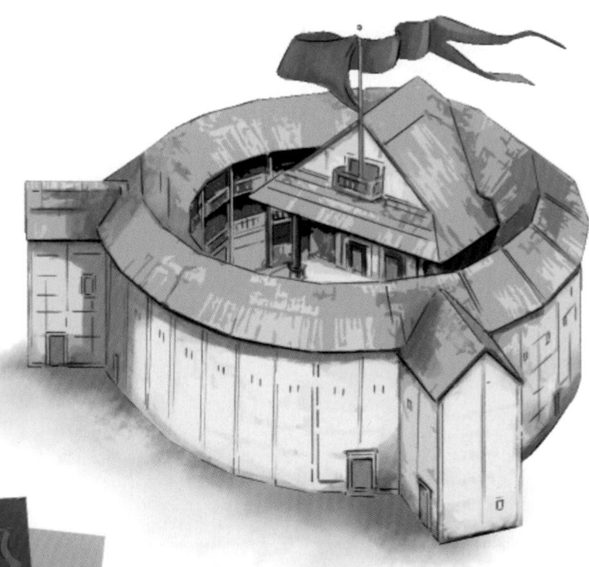

First Night

Opening in 1599, *Julius Caesar* was most likely the first of Shakespeare's plays to be performed at the Globe Theater, which was owned by the theater company that Shakespeare wrote for most of his life—the Lord Chamberlain's Men.

Killer Casting

Before becoming one of the most famous assassins in history, for the theater shooting of American President Abraham Lincoln, John Wilkes Booth played Mark Antony in a production of the play in 1864.

Dare To Be Different

In direct contrast to the theater culture that saw its inception, where all the characters were played by men, 2012 saw an all-female production of the play; it also saw an all-black production performed by the Royal Shakespeare Company.

CAESAR... DID YOU KNOW?

Royal Vanity: After Julius Caesar was declared dictator for life, it is widely believed that he started wearing his crown all the time, so that he could conceal his receding hairline.

Pirates: As a young man, Caesar was once captured by pirates. He befriended his captors and joked with them that once he was released he would arrange to have them all caught and executed. They all laughed, until he was released, and he proceeded to do just that.

Overkill: Julius Caesar was stabbed a total of 23 times before he fell to his assassins. They apparently wanted to ensure the man stayed dead.

Conqueror's Humility: In 45 B.C., Caesar changed the name of the Roman month of Quintilis to Julius, thus giving us the month of July.

About the Author

THE MAKING OF WILLIAM SHAKESPEARE'S JULIUS CAESAR

For those of you who want to know more about what happens behind the scenes here at Campfire, get ready for a whirlwind tour of our studio!

1 First up, we finalize the script. After making sure it's got everything our readers demand, such as pace, style, and drama, we hand it over to the artist.

PAGE: 62

PANEL 1

[TO THE ARTIST: Medium close-up on Mark Antony. Head bowed, one hand clasped to his chest as if in pain.]

ANTONY: Bear with me...

ANTONY: My heart is in the coffin there with Caesar, and I must pause till it come back to me.

PANEL 2

[TO THE ARTIST: A group shot of our citizen commentators, all gesticulating excitedly and engaged in enthusiastic conversation.]

CITIZEN 1: Methinks there is much reason in his sayings.

CITIZEN 2: If thou consider rightly of the matter, Caesar has had great wrong.

CITIZEN 4: Mark'd ye his words? He would not take the crown; therefore 'tis certain he was not ambitious..

PANEL 3

[TO THE ARTIST: A small panel, the first of four in succession. If they can be fitted across the page in a single row, that would be great. Close up on the first citizen, looking angry.]

CITIZEN 1: If it be found so, some will dear abide it!

PANEL 4

[TO THE ARTIST: A small panel. Close-up on the second citizen, looking sad.]

CITIZEN 2: Poor soul, his eyes are red as fire with weeping!

PANEL 5

[TO THE ARTIST: A small panel. Close up on third citizen, nodding in agreement.]

CITIZEN 3: There's not a nobler man in Rome than Mark Antony.

PANEL 6

[TO THE ARTIST: A small panel. Close up on fourth citizen, looking up expectantly.]

CITIZEN 4: Now mark him, he begins again to speak.

2 The artist then starts drawing up the pages, dividing each scene into a series of panels.

3 When the artist has finished a page it is given to one of our colorists, who will then help bring the book to life with an explosion of color.

4 So far we've got some great colored artwork but no words on the page. This is the job of the letterer who will now add in all the word balloons, thought bubbles, and sound effects.

5 Then our editorial team will go over the page, making sure that everything is picture perfect before sending the book on to the printers, who prepare what you are reading right now!

In the reign of King Duncan, Scotland is a just and hospitable land, with loyal, warlike thanes guarding the best interests of the people, until the very best among them, Macbeth, gives in to a fatal temptation and commits regicide. But will the crown of Scotland sit easy on his head? Or will justice be restored?

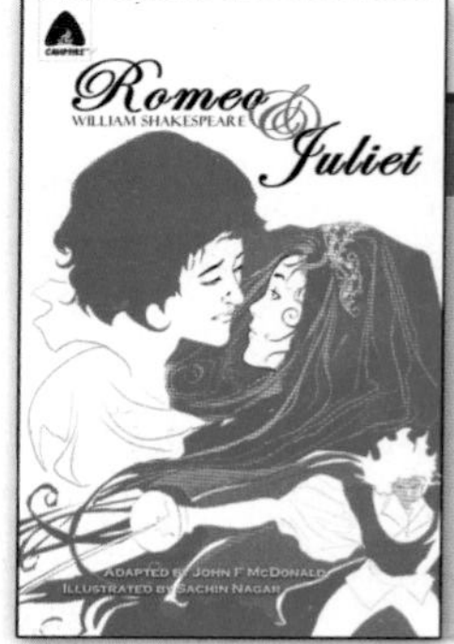

The intense hatred between the Montagues and the Capulets is well known in Verona. Yet love blossoms between Romeo and Juliet, the children of these two families. A brawl between the kinsmen of the Houses leads to Romeo's exile, and from then on events spin out of control leading ultimately to tragedy.

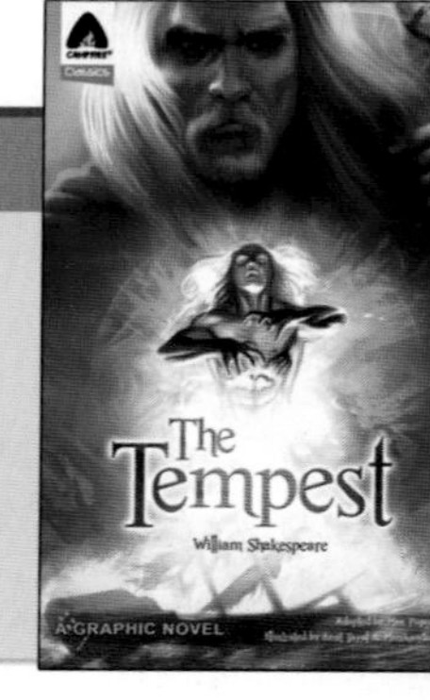

Although Shakespeare's final play, *The Tempest* is filled with the supernatural, its message is that real magic lies in the emotions of the human heart. In this stunning drama, love blossoms, the enslaved are freed, old friends are reunited and the chilling vengeance of a wronged man is calmed and soothed.

The Merchant of Venice has everything to make it one of the most dramatic romantic comedies of all time. Antonio, a young Venetian merchant borrows money from Shylock, a shrewd moneylender. But when he has trouble repaying his debt, Shylock devises a vicious retribution.